Welcome

Check out my other books
on amazon.ca

Madison's Journey
Colin's Path

Destiny Falls

Prologue

Large pellets of rain dented the bright blue umbrella that Callie Anderson held over top of the wild, red curls of her wind-blown hair. The wind had died down but the sky was still watering the land with it's tears on this somber October morning. As Callie peeked around the blue fabric and up at the dark, gray clouds looming above her, she thought that it was a fitting day to be standing amongst the gravestones in this quiet cemetery. Her eyes, then roamed around surroundings until they landed on a large gathering of darkly clad mourners on the far side of the cemetery. Her heart sank as she observed their bowed heads and grief-stricken bodies. Her gaze lingered on them for a moment before turning back to focus on the gray gravestone in front of her.

Staring at the large gray stone, her head bowed slightly as she read the encryption etched onto its face. "Pops, Father, Husband, Best friend." The feeling of sorrow that always accompanied her to this place, began to envelope her as she swallowed the sob forming in her throat. "I miss you so much, Pops. But I did it. I got my certification and a job. A real job, in the service department at one of those fancy dealerships, just like we talked about." As a small, proud smile touched the corners of her lips, she felt the sorrow give way to a small sensation of joy and pride. "I couldn't believe it when they told me that the job was mine. I was sure it would take longer but I did it; for you." Leaning her head back, Callie peered around the umbrella, to once again stare into the depths of the dark sky. "I hope I make you proud up there, Pops!" A single tear slipped down her cheek as she focused her gaze back to the gravestone. She stood staring at it in silence for a long time, thinking about her grandfather and then, after blowing him a kiss, she touched the stone, closed her eyes and said a silent prayer before taking slow, heavy steps away from his grave.

Several tears slipped down her cheeks as she strolled, with slumped shoulders, down the cobble stone pathway that would lead her to the parking lot. As her footsteps led her closer to the gathered group of mourners, she watched them as they slowly began to step away from their gathering place. She stopped a respectful distance away to allow them their privacy as they shuffled towards their cars. Many of them were holding tissues to their eyes as they held on to each other, crying silently. Callie was quiet as she stepped to the side of the path, trying to make herself as invisible as possible, not wanting to interrupt their mourning. As she stood silently, her eyes wandered towards the patch of grass where the mourners had been gathered, landing on a tall man in a dark suit who was still standing beside the open grave. He was holding the hand of a blond, pigtailed little girl, who stood as tall as the man's hip. The girl was fidgeting beside him but the man seemed to be oblivious to it as he stared into the dark hole in front of him. After a few moments, the man knelt in front of the girl, wrapped her in his arms and held her for a long time. When he finally released her, he remained crouched down in front of her. Callie's focus stayed on the two strangers, unable to draw her eyes away from them. After a moment, she watched a smile touch the little girl's lips as she nodded, prompting the man to stand up. The man gazed down at the hole one more time and then spoke to the little girl, who raised her hand to her mouth and blew a kiss towards the open grave. The man then, scooped the girl into his arms and began marching towards the parking lot. Callie's heart sank and a fresh feeling of sorrow washed over her as she realized that the young girl was saying good-bye to her mother. She kept her eyes on the pair as they approached the group of people waiting for them. Hugs and tears were exchanged as she continued to observe them and then the group slowly climbed into their waiting vehicles.

Callie stayed planted to her spot as she watched the cars drive away; her heart aching for the strangers. She felt a connection to the young girl and now as she stood watching the group leave, her entire body ached with sadness. But as she felt that sadness wash over her, she quickly shook her head. "You are being ridiculous. You don't even know those people." Sighing sadly, with her eyes still lingering on the cars leaving the cemetery, she responded in quiet sorrow, to her previous statement. "Yes, but you know what it's like to lose your mother." As those words left her lips, she turned her eyes to the open grave in the distance, staring at it for a long time, before eventually making her way back to the Impala waiting for her in the parking lot. Driving home, Callie's heart was still enveloped in sadness and for the rest of the day, she found herself thinking about that man and his daughter.

Chapter 1

****Four Years Later****

The narrow streets of the quiet town where Callie called home, were bare as she pressed the pink, leather boot cradling her right foot down against the gas pedal. Whizzing through the streets of her sleepy neighbourhood induced a rush of adrenaline to shoot through her as a wide smile touched the corners of her pink, glittering lips and a twinkle shone in her light-brown eyes. Although the sun had set hours earlier leaving only white stars twinkling against the backdrop of the dark, December night, bright Christmas lights adorning every house brightened the night around her as they reflected off the fresh blanket of white snow layering the ground. The slippery snow underneath her tires was making for an enjoyable drive as the speedometer of the black, 67' Impala slowly inched higher and higher, prompting her heart to thump excitedly against her chest. She expertly maneuvered the classic car through the narrow streets, drifting around corners as the tires slid along the slippery patches of snow. Each time the back end of the car fish-tailed, Callie's smile widened. After turning the corner onto the street where her house sat, she pressed a little harder on the gas and as the speedometer sailed above the posted speed limit, Callie noticed the shadow of a car hiding in a dark corner of the street. Her heart constricted when she realized that it was no ordinary car, and as the blue and red lights on its roof began to shine brightly in her rear-view mirror, Callie cursed under her breath. She slowed the Impala down and pulled to the side of the road, shaking her head at the fact that she had just been pulled over, only two houses from her own home. Reaching into the glove box, she pulled out her registration papers and was just grabbing her driver's license from the wallet resting on the passenger seat, when a light tap rapped against the window beside her.

She slowly unrolled the window with the lever glancing upwards as she did. Recognizing the face of the uniform-clad officer hovering above her, a small smile touched the corners of Callie's lips. As her eyes rested on the handsome, chiseled face that had been invading her thoughts for days, she felt a flutter dance across her chest. "Officer Pierce."

The officer's lips were curled downwards but as soon as Callie spoke his name, recognition flashed in his eyes, bringing a touch of a smile to his lips. "Miss Anderson, small world." Amusement enveloped his words and laughter danced in his eyes, prompting Callie to cringe, as the smile framing her lips curled into a sheepish grin.

Handing him her papers, she swallowed hard. "How is your night going, Officer?"

Officer Pierce stared down at her with a smirk playing across his lips. When he spoke, amusement was still evident in his voice. "Better than yours." He then tilted his head and raised an eyebrow in her direction. "Or maybe not. What had you driving so fast?"

For a split second, Callie contemplated making up an excuse but instead she slumped her shoulders and hung her head down slightly. "Nothing." She then tapped the steering wheel in front of her. "This old gal just likes to fly." Her reply initiated a chuckle to fly out of the Officer's mouth, prompting her to raise her eyes back up to meet his and the moment their eyes met all hint of amusement vanished from his features.

"I'm sure she does but you're gonna hurt someone,

8

probably yourself if you keep that up." The amusement in his voice had been replaced with sternness, and was layered with a tone of concern.

"I'm sorry Officer." Her words were genuine as apology flickered in her eyes. They locked eyes for a moment before Officer Pierce cleared his throat and let his eyes fall to the papers in his hand, which he quickly thrust back through the window.

"Okay, well, I'll let you go with a warning this time, but Miss Anderson?"

"Yes?"

His dark eyes softened as they sparkled under the light of the street lamp that loomed above them. "Do slow down and be more careful. Wouldn't want anything to happen to you, would we?"

Callie's heart flip flopped at the kindness of his words and the gentleness of his voice and then she felt her pulse begin to race as his dark gray eyes locked onto hers. She nodded but didn't speak as Officer Pierce turned and strolled with long, quick steps, back to his patrol car. She watched him from the side mirror and just as he reached his car door, she stuck her head out the window.

"Thank you, Officer. Have a good rest of your night. And be safe out there."

He turned back towards her and she saw his lips curl upwards, revealing the most amazing smile she had ever seen. She watched as he waved and then climb back into his car before she settled against the seat in her own vehicle. Leaning her head against the head rest she took a moment to allow her pulse to return to normal. As she sat in her vehicle, her eyes wandered to the rear-view mirror and she watched Officer Pierce with his head down, working in his car. When he looked up, she quickly diverted her eyes from the mirror, and then started the car, gliding it forward slowly until she was parked, safely in her driveway. When she climbed out of the car, her gaze was drawn towards Officer Pierce's patrol car, which was still parked on the side of the road. Walking up the pathway to her front door, she glanced at his patrol car one more time before stepping into the darkness of her drafty, old home, and as she did, she wondered if he was watching her too.

Chapter 2

Landon stared at the Impala as it pulled into a driveway two houses from where he had just been standing and talking to it's beautiful, red-headed driver. He had been too distracted by her dazzling smile and sparkling light brown eyes to notice her address when he had been holding her driver's license in his hand. Surprise had enveloped him when it was her beautiful smile greeting him from the speeding Impala; he didn't think that after their first encounter he would ever see her again. And since that first meeting, three nights earlier, he hadn't been able to get her out of his mind. As he watched her jean clad hips sway towards the white front door of the large, Victorian home, his mind wandered back to that first meeting.

"Miss, can I see some ID please?" The chatter of bar patrons mixed with loud music made it necessary for Landon to lean in close to her and raise his voice slightly as he stood in a corner of the crowded bar.

The gorgeous red head standing in front of him sighed and rolled her eyes. "Seriously? Are you arresting me? I was just defending myself." Concern enveloped her questions and began to flicker in her eyes as she glanced over her shoulder at the young man who had a towel pressed against his nose. The towel was slowly turning a bright shade of red as his friends circled around him, laughing. When the red head brought her eyes back to meet Landon's, the concern in them had vanished and anger was beginning to brew within them. Her movement was exaggerated by her anger as she motioned her arm towards the young man. "That jerk, grabbed my ass more than once. I warned him after the second time that I'd break his face if he did it again."

Landon nodded, trying not to smile at her description of events or at the fierceness with which she spoke. "I guess he didn't believe you."

Their eyes locked then and, Landon felt his pulse quicken as he got lost in her beautiful brown eyes. They stood in silence for a moment before he remembered why he was here. "I'm not arresting you, Miss Anderson. I've spoken to all the witnesses and they substantiated your story, you were protecting yourself. I just need your information for my file."

Her eyes narrowed on him, a residual of anger still flashing within them. "File? If you aren't arresting me, why do you need a file?"

Landon glanced from her to the young man with the towel and then back to her. "Because, we're arresting him. Multiple women have issued sexual harassment complaints against him."

He watched her big brown eyes grow wide as the anger within them was replaced with shock. "Really?" Disbelief clouded her one-word question.

Landon nodded. "Yes, apparently, you weren't the first woman at this club tonight that his hands couldn't help but wander towards. He'll be charged with sexual harassment and possible assault."

Callie nodded; her eyes still wide. "Wow. What about me?"

"What about you?"

"Well, I did break his nose."

Landon's lips curled upwards. "Yes, you did. Nice shot." When a surprised laugh exploded from Miss

Anderson's lips Landon shook his head and leaned in, lowering his voice as he spoke. "Don't tell anyone I said that."

She laughed softly and then drew a cross over her heart with her fingers. "Cross my heart."

Her promise prompted them both to shake with laughter before Landon cleared his throat again. "Okay, so ID please and then I can have one of the officer's drive you home if you like?"

Miss Anderson quickly shook her head in response. "No, I'm good. I already called a car." She glanced down at her phone. "It'll be here in a few minutes."

Landon nodded as she handed him her ID. "Okay." As his eyes landed on her right hand, he noticed that it was starting to swell and was quickly turning a bright shade of red. "And you should put some ice on that when you get home. It's gonna be sore for a few days."

Miss Anderson's eyes dropped down to the hand in question. "Yeah, but it was worth it."

The corners of Landon's mouth curved upwards as she raised twinkling eyes back up to meet his. They held each other's gaze for a moment and then he took a reluctant step backwards. "Take care, Miss Anderson."

Her lips curled upwards, revealing the most beautiful smile he had ever seen; it stretched up to her eyes, illuminating her entire face. "You too, Officer Pierce. Stay safe out there."

Landon nodded, and took one last look at her, allowing his eyes to briefly move up and down her body. She was tall, only a few inches shorter than *himself, probably due to the heeled wedges strapped to her feet. The white floral dress that clung to her hips, dipped down to reveal just enough cleavage to keep a guy distracted imagining what lied beneath the fabric. Landon's pulse quickened again as his eyes lingered on her body and when he pulled his eyes back up to hers, there was a twinkle shimmering in her eyes. He immediately felt heat rising in his body, so he quickly turned around without uttering another word and strode with quick steps towards his partner.*

Shaking his head, thinking about that night, Landon brought his focus back to the present. He focused his gaze on her front door but she had disappeared into the house by then. A wave of disappointment washed over him prompting him to immediately shake his head. He stared at his reflection in the rear-view mirror while scolding himself out loud. "What's wrong with you? You don't even know her and she's way too young for you. But she's feisty and beautiful and just like…" He shook his head again. "No, don't go there. You can't compare everyone you meet to Iz. No one is Iz. But that beautiful red-head is…" He closed his eyes for a moment and when he opened them again, he stared at himself in the mirror one more time. "A stranger." His voice was defiant, like he was fighting with himself and trying to convince himself of something. Shaking his head again, he started the car and pulled away, using all of his will power to keep himself from looking for her as he drove, slowly past her house.

Chapter 3

"I can't believe that after today we get a whole two weeks off." Jade, one of Callie's co-workers had just taken a seat beside Callie at their usual table in the lunchroom. Callie and Jade had become fast friends in the six months since Jade had taken over as the loans officer at the dealership. Along with Sully, the dealerships amazing receptionist, who was the third member of their tiny lunch group, they were the lone females working in the building and therefore tended to stick together at lunch time.

"Me too." Callie said between bites of her grilled chicken salad as she surveyed the lunchroom. It was a fair-sized room with six large round tables, and a small kitchen area consisting of a sink, a few cupboards and a large stainless-steel fridge. "Where's Sully?" Curiosity surrounded Callie's question as her gaze landed on Jade.

Jade, who was busy unpacking her lunch, shook her head, a wide grin quickly spreading across her bright red lips. "She didn't come in today, started her Christmas break early. Debbie had her baby last night."

Callie's eyes widened and her mouth dropped open. "What? How am I just hearing about this now?"

Laughter shook Jade's shoulders as she shrugged. "I have no idea, babe. It's probably because the only time you leave the grease pit is for lunch." Amusement framed Jade's words and a twinkle sparkled in her oval shaped, sky-blue eyes.

Jade's reply prompted laughter to float out of Callie's mouth. "Fair enough. But in my defense, the one and only time I came to your office, I left a grease stain on your chair and was banished from ever entering your sanctuary again."

Jade's eyebrows lifted upwards as she glanced at Callie. "My sanctuary, eh?" Laughter danced in her eyes as she continued. "Well, I'm sorry, but I don't think our customers would like to leave my office with a giant grease patch on their butts, do you?"

Callie giggled and shook her head. "No, probably not." The women, then exchanged amused glances as Jade nodded.

After swallowing another bite of her dressing smothered salad, Callie turned questioning eyes back up in Jade's direction. "So, are you gonna tell me? Boy or girl?"

Jade glanced up from her lunch, surprise flashing across her face until understanding registered in her eyes. "Oh, a little boy. Eight pounds, nine ounces. Both he and mama are doing well. He was born this morning just after five. And Sully is ecstatic."

Callie grinned widely as joy for Sully enveloped her heart. "I bet. First grand-baby and all. I can't wait to buy him his first wrench set."

Jade, who had just taken a sip of her soda, laughed, spraying soda all over the table, prompting a giggle to escape Callie's lips

"Nice! That was very lady like, missy."

Grabbing some napkins, Jade wiped the table and her face before turning an annoyed grin on Callie. "Well, it was your fault. Who buys a baby a wrench set?"

Callie giggled again. "I didn't say I was buying it now. I may not know much about babies, but I do know enough to know that they don't use wrench sets." Laughter surrounded them again, and after that, they sat quietly and finished their meals.

Just as they were packing up to return to their respective work stations, Jade tilted her head in Callie's direction as a shadow of sadness crept into the corners of her eyes. "So, what are you doing for Christmas? Are you going to be alone?" Concern was evident in Jade's voice.

As Callie's eyes landed on Jade, she felt a slight hitch in her heart as she thought about Christmas' of the past with her grandfather. Sighing, she responded quietly. "Yeah, but it's okay, I'm used to it. Since Pops died it's been just me." Jade nodded and as she did, Callie watched the shadow of sadness in Jade's eyes grow into concern. Callie quickly shook her head and placed a reassuring hand on Jade's arm. "Don't worry about me Jadey. I'll be fine. I usually volunteer at the church down the street from my house on Christmas. They serve Christmas dinner to the homeless."

Callie's words did nothing to alleviate the concern in Jade's eyes. "Callie…"

Callie, wanting to end this conversation quickly, shook her head, while smiling brightly across the table. "Jade, seriously. I'll be fine. You go and enjoy your family. When do you leave for the cabin?" Jade had been talking about her family Christmas for months now and as the days of December flew by, Jade's excitement had increased exponentially. Every year, Jade's parents, her older brother and his family, her older sister and her family and Jade and Elliott, Jade's fiancé, spend Christmas at their cabin in the mountains. Jade explained it as the perfect Christmas, complete with all the snow they could ever want. Jade's description of her family Christmas had often left Callie feeling lonely, but she would never burden Jade with that truth.

Jade didn't respond to Callie's inquiry, and as her silence grew, Callie could see an idea forming in Jade's eyes and as it did, a wide smile began to spread across Jade's lips. "You should come with us. Oh my god…yes…that's a great idea." Jade's voice was loud and filled with enthusiasm and several of their co-workers turned to stare at them from neighbouring tables. But Jade didn't seem to notice or care about their stares, she was too excited by her idea. "Seriously, Callie. That would be so amazing."

Callie immediately shook her head. "No, Jade, I can't. I mean, I wouldn't want to intrude on your family."

"You wouldn't be intruding. It's Christmas, the more the merrier. And besides, when my mom finds out that you're spending Christmas alone, she's going to insist that you join us."

Callie laughed softly; she knew that Jade was right about that. Jade's mother, Courtney, whom Callie had met a few times, was a force of nature. She was the movie version of a perfect, yet meddlesome mother, who loved her children and didn't mind telling them what she thought about their every move. And she was a fabulous cook who made the most delicious cinnamon buns Callie had ever tasted. Shaking her head, Callie responded to Jade, a smirk touching the corners of her mouth. "Well, don't tell your mother then."

Laughter danced in Jade's eyes as she grinned widely, tilting her head in Callie's direction. "Yeah, that's not gonna happen. So, you have two choices; agree to come with us or deal with my mother." Callie laughed again while shaking her head and as she did, Jade grabbed her phone from the table and began tapping the screen.

"What are you doing?"

Jade glanced up with mischief twinkling in her eyes. "Calling my mother."

Callie's eyes grew wide. "What? Are you serious?"

"As a heart attack."

Callie shook her head, a small smile touching her lips. But concern quickly flashed in her eyes, prompting Jade to stop what she was doing, lean forward and place her hands over top of Callie's. "Seriously, Callie, I don't want you to spend another Christmas alone. The cabin is big enough. Mom and dad did an expansion a few

19

years ago, so even with the grandkids, there's plenty of room."

Callie shook her head, uncertainty flashing in her eyes. "I don't know. What about your brother and sister? How would they feel about a stranger crashing their Christmas?"

"Well first of all, you aren't a stranger and secondly they won't care. Like I said, the more the merrier." Jade's eyes were pleading with Callie to say yes as she spoke and as much as Callie felt that she should say no, a huge part of her wanted to say yes. It had been a long time since she had spent Christmas with anyone and even when her grandfather was alive, Christmas was usually just the two of them and a couple of her grandfather's buddies. As Callie thought more about Jade's offer, excitement at the prospect of a real family Christmas began to bubble up within her.

"And you're sure no one will mind?"

Jade shook her head as her eyes began to shine. "Yes, I'm sure. And to make you feel better, I'll finish my call and double check with mom. Okay?"

Callie nodded and then watched as an excited Jade played with her phone before placing it against her ear.

"Hey mom." Jade smiled across the table as she listened to her mother. "Yes, mom. Elliott and I will be on the road first thing Sunday morning. I'm done work at four tonight and then we're gonna finish our shopping tomorrow before hitting the road." She paused and then rolled her

20

eyes as she listened again. Callie laughed as Jade, then rolled her eyes a second time. "I won't forget the tree mom." Another pause. "Yes, we're keeping it watered. It'll be fine mom, we do it every year." Another pause. "Yes, of course. Now can you take a breath so I can tell you why I called." That last sentence prompted laughter to escape Callie's throat as she listened to Jade continue. "I was wondering if you would mind another guest joining us." Another short pause. "Yes, Callie. How did you know that?" She listened again and a wide grin spread across her lips. "Oh, mother's intuition, eh?" Jade rolled her eyes at Callie and they both giggled quietly. "Yeah, no, she doesn't have any family and…" Jade stopped, and Callie knew that Courtney had interrupted. "That's exactly what I told her. Okay, great. Thanks mom." Another pause. "Yeah, for the whole two weeks. She'll come up with Elliott and I." Jade gave Callie a thumbs up sign and Callie could feel butterflies begin to fly around in her stomach; a combination of both nervous and excited butterflies, she was sure.

Jade hung up a few minutes later and she was beaming when her eyes focused on Callie. "Okay, we're all set. Mom's gonna get your room ready and Elliott and I will pick you up on Sunday morning. Bring warm clothes and a few nice things cause we dress up for Christmas dinner and New Year's Eve. And bring your dancing shoes."

Callie's eyes widened. "Dancing shoes? New Year's Eve?"

"Yup. We're gonna be up there for the whole two weeks of Christmas break."

Callie shook her head as doubt began to creep into her eyes and a small knot began to form in her stomach. "Jade, maybe this isn't…"

Jade shook her head as she locked her eyes on to Callie's. "Nope. Too late. You're coming." And then, with that stated, Jade stood up. "Now, let's get back to it. Only three more hours until we are officially on holiday!"

Callie laughed as Jade grabbed her hand and led her out of the lunchroom. After changing back into her grease-stained coveralls, Callie got to work on her last car of the day, and just over four hours later, she was heading home in her matted black 67' Impala. She was sure to stay under the posted speed limit in order to not attract the attentions of a certain gorgeous police officer. As her thoughts wandered to Officer Pierce, she couldn't stop the smile that spread across her lips but just as quickly as the smile formed, it slanted downwards as Callie's thoughts quickly turned to her plans for the next two weeks. As excited as she was at the prospect of a big family Christmas, she couldn't help feeling like she would be an intruder.

She quickly shook her head, trying to rid her mind of that thought. "Stop. If you keep thinking like that, you are going to be miserable for the next two weeks. Just enjoy it. You'll eat some yummy food, make some memories and it won't be so bad." She then glanced at herself in the rear-view mirror. "You know you want to have a real Christmas for once and Pops would be so happy for you. So quit worrying about it. Jade is amazing, so the rest of her family is probably great too." Grinning at the reflection in the mirror, she ended her pep talk and although the reflection still looked skeptical, she straightened her shoulders and tried to feel confident as she drove home through the snow-covered streets.

The following day, Callie climbed up into the attic, grabbed the old suitcase that had belonged to her grandmother and hauled it downstairs. However, upon further inspection, in the bright lights of her sunny living room, Callie realized that the suitcase was no longer suitable for use. The zipper was broken and there was a hole in the bottom of it. As she stared at the old, unusable suitcase she decided that her only course of action was to go to the mall and buy something new, so she grabbed her coat, and her purse and marched swiftly to the Impala.

Once at the mall, it dawned on Callie that she hadn't been to the mall since the Christmas decorations had gone up. As she strolled through the crowds of people that were finishing their Christmas shopping lists, she took a moment to enjoy the decorations that littered the walls around her. The displays in the windows of the stores were adorned with snowmen, Santa's, snow and beautiful Christmas trees. Strolling along the tiled floor, she stopped when she noticed Santa's village. The village consisted of a blue painted building with a sign above the door that read 'Santa's Workshop' and fake snow on its roof. Fake snow was also spread around the yard of the village and ornament covered trees and brightly wrapped presents were displayed throughout the rest of the village. As it was a Saturday, children were lined up for their chance to sit on Santa's knee. Callie watched for a few minutes as children were escorted by a woman dressed up like Mrs. Claus towards a very authentic looking Kris Kringle, who was sitting in a large, green velvet chair. Her lips curled upwards at the joy displayed on a young boy's face as he spoke animatedly to Santa. The sight of it created a flow of warmth through her body as memories of her own visits to Santa's Village with her grandfather suddenly flooded her mind. As she thought about those happy moments, joy spread through her body and when she turned away from the scene, she was feeling enveloped in Christmas spirit. Within minutes of leaving Santa's Village, Callie found the store she was looking for and quickly purchased a new suitcase for her adventure to Jade's family's cabin. After accomplishing her mission, she decided to wander through the rest of the mall, thinking that it might be nice to show up to the cabin with a gift for Jade's parents. And two hours later, Callie left the mall with an armful of bags, a few gifts for Jade's family and a few new outfits for herself since most of her clothes were covered in grease stains from her weekends of tinkering with the Impala. When she returned home, she was feeling pretty good about her day and about her plans for the next two weeks. Santa and Mrs. Clause had helped her connect with her Christmas spirit and as she wrapped her gifts and packed her suitcase, she hummed Christmas carols as excitement for her unexpected Christmas plans began to build up within her.

Chapter 4

At precisely eight the following morning, exactly one week before Christmas, Callie was climbing into the back of Elliott's shiny, red, extended cab F-150. The interior of the truck was leather and so fancy that as Callie clicked herself into the seat belt, she felt a little out of place. She was wearing her well worn, pink, fur-lined winter coat, over faded denim jeans and plain black t-shirt. The pink winter boots on her feet, were functional, not fancy and as she looked around the posh pick-up and then at both Elliott and Jade, a knot began to form in her stomach as the feeling that this was a mistake began to overwhelm her. Jade, was dressed as immaculately as she usually was. Her hair was pulled back into a perfect bun on the top of her head, a complete contrast to Callie's loose, messy curls. The fancy beige coat that hung over Jade's dark dress pants gave one the impression that she was a model who had just stepped off the cover of a magazine. Elliott was dressed similarly and if Callie didn't know better, she would have thought that he was a model straight out of GQ magazine.

As anxiety began to envelope her, Callie tried to smooth the red curls that rested on her shoulders. At work, she always wore her hair in a ponytail, but outside of work hours she preferred to allow it to be loose and free. Normally she thought that her hair was one of her best features, but today staring at the back of Jade's perfect head of dark hair, Callie's self doubt began to take over and she found herself shrinking slightly in her seat.

She was still staring at the back of Jade's head, worrying about her outfit and how she would fit in with Jade's family when both of her companions turned around in their seats, resting their bright smiling eyes on her.

"You look great Callie. It's always nice to see you out of those coveralls. You look like a woman for a change."

Callie smiled at Jade's comment but Elliott's eyes grew wide and he gently hit Jade's arm. "Jadey, that's awful."

Jade turned her attention to her fiancé. "What? It's true. You wouldn't believe how well Callie fits in with the guys. I think most of us forget that she's not one of them half the time. All I meant, was that it's nice to see her in pretty girl clothes."

Callie's lips stayed curled upwards and she sat straightened up in her seat at Jade's kind words.

When Jade turned her gaze back to Callie, Callie tilted her head. "Well, I wouldn't say my clothes are pretty. Look at you. You always look like a model."

A light shade of red began to creep onto Jade's cheeks and Callie watched as Elliott smiled with loving and appreciative eyes at his bride to be.

"I wouldn't say a model." Embarrassment enveloped Jade's words prompting Callie to shake her head.

"I would." She then turned her focus to Elliott. "And you too. You look like one of those GQ models. You guys look stunning together."

Both Elliott and Jade smiled appreciatively at Callie and then turned loving eyes on each other. After a moment, Elliott turned his attention to the world in front of him. "Well, I think both of you ladies look lovely. So, what do you say, lovely ladies? Shall we hit the road?"

Callie grinned and nodded as Jade turned her attention frontwards and placed her hand on Elliott's shoulder. "Yes, sir." She then looked over her shoulder to offer Callie a smile before turning her attention to the dashboard. "And I made us a play-list for the drive. An hour and a half of Christmas carols." Jade practically sung her last sentence prompting Callie to giggle at her enthusiasm.

The drive north to Jade's family cabin in the mountains was the most scenic drive Callie had ever been on. They only spent about ten minutes on the freeway before turning onto a side road. As they climbed up the mountain road, the snow on the trees and on the side, embankments got thicker and thicker and as the sun rose higher in the sky, the ice crystals of the snowflakes resting on the trees glistened brightly all around them. It was one of the most beautiful sights Callie had ever seen. Taking her phone out of her handbag, she snapped a few pics capturing Jade's attention from the front seat as she did.

"It's beautiful, isn't it?" Jade's red lips curled upwards as Callie set her wide, twinkling eyes on her friend.

"The most beautiful view I've ever seen. I've never been up this mountain before."

Jade's oval eyes grew wide and her lips formed a surprised 'o'. "Seriously? But haven't you lived in Crescent Falls your whole life?"

"Yeah, but Pops and I didn't really venture too far from home. The farthest we ever traveled was to Westwood to browse the auto wreckers." Callie grinned and Jade laughed lightly.

"Well, then I'm glad you came. You deserve this." The kindness in Jade's voice prompted a shy smile to pass across Callie's lips as Jade reached back and squeezed Callie's hand. "And don't be nervous. My family is great, they won't bite, I promise."

Callie laughed and so did Elliott who set his eyes on Callie through the rear-view mirror. "That is unless you're the one dating their baby girl."

His reply prompted Jade to let go of Callie's hand and turn her attention to her fiancé. She fluttered her eyelashes while addressing him with soft, sweet words. "But I'm worth every scar, aren't I?"

Nodding immediately, Elliott turned his sparkling eyes on Jade. "Absolutely."

All three of them laughed at his response and Callie stared at the two of them, as a feeling of warmth began to envelope her. She was still nervous about spending two weeks with strangers but if Jade's family was anything like Jade and Elliott, Callie knew she was going to feel right at home. Settling back into her seat, she felt her whole body relax as she focused on the scenery flying past her window. And then, before she knew it, they were pulling into a long, snow-packed driveway.

Jade turned back with bright shining eyes and a wide joyous smile touching her lips. "We're here."

Callie grinned at the happiness in Jade's eyes and then as she gazed out the windshield, over Jade's shoulder, her eyes grew into wide saucers. "Holy crap!"

At Callie's shocked words, Jade turned her eyes to focus on what had drawn Callie's attention as a happy smile touched her lips. "I know right? You were probably expecting a small log cabin."

Callie didn't speak, she couldn't, she was too shocked to say anything, instead she just nodded in agreement.

"Well, I didn't want to scare you so I told you it was a cabin. Which it is, or was, I guess. Now it's more like a..."

"Mansion?" Callie's voice was quiet with shock as she finished Jade's sentence.

Laughter enveloped both Jade and Elliott as Elliott responded. "That was my first reaction too. But wait until you get inside. It really does have a mountain cabin feel to it."

Callie nodded but she couldn't tear her eyes away from the home in front of her. When Jade had mentioned that her family owned a cabin in the mountains, she had imagined a little log cabin, but this was no little log cabin. It was made of logs but it was the size of at least four log cabins, each with two stories and a large deck that spanned the entire length of the top floor. As Callie continued to stare at the structure in front of her, Jade and Elliott climbed out of the truck and it wasn't until Jade pulled the passenger door open, that Callie finally tore her gaze away from the cabin.

As Jade stepped aside to allow Callie to slide out, Callie shook her head. "Wow, Jade. I don't know what to say. This is amazing."

Jade offered Callie a wide, appreciative smile. "Thanks. Just wait until you see inside. Elliott's right, it really does have that log cabin feel, especially at Christmas. My mom is a Christmas fanatic and there isn't a surface in the cabin that isn't covered in some sort of Christmas decor."

Callie grinned at that, feeling excitement begin to course through her body. Her and her grandfather hadn't been much for decorating after her grandmother's passing. Usually they got a tree, hung some stockings and called it a day. Callie couldn't wait to see what was in store for her inside this cabin. She took one more look at the beautiful structure in front of her before joining Elliott and Jade at the back of the truck to help unload. As she did, she glanced at the world around her, and felt joy ripple through her body. Trees glistening with snow surrounded the large yard and as a smile of happiness touched her lips, she took a long, deep breath in. The air was crisp and smelled like fresh snow and pine trees. After taking a few moments to enjoy the scent of the mountain air, Callie turned her attention back to the bags in the truck and as she did, she heard the sound of a man's voice echoing from the front of the house.

"You made it!"

At the sound of the voice, Jade turned on her heel and scrambled towards the man. Callie peered around the truck to see a tall man with silver hair and a silver beard grinning widely at Jade. Within seconds Jade had flung herself into the man's arms and he had his arms wrapped tightly around her with a joyous smile spread across his face. The scene brought a tear to Callie's eye as thoughts of her grandfather floated through her mind.

After releasing each other, Jade and the man strolled towards the back of the truck. "Daddy, this is Callie. Callie, this is my father, Nicholas."

Nicholas, who was a tall, wide shouldered man,

grinned happily down at Callie, extending his hand towards her. She grasped his large, wrinkled hand with her own and smiled politely as she stared into his sparkling sky-blue eyes, which were the same colour as Jade's. "It's nice to meet you, Nicholas."

"Please, it's Nick. And the pleasure is all mine, dear. I'm so glad you could join us."

Warmth spread through Callie's body at the kindness in his voice. "Thank you for letting me crash your family Christmas."

"Nonsense." Nick's voice was loud but genuine. "The more the merrier. And besides, any friend of Jade's is automatically family."

Callie's lips curled upwards as Nick turned his attention to Elliott. "Here, son, let me help you with those." Nick then set his eyes back on Jade. "Jade, you two go inside. Your mother can't wait to show Callie around."

Light laughter shook Jade's shoulders as she rolled her eyes before linking her arm with Callie's and leading Callie towards the cabin. "Come on, better get this over with."

"Over with?" Confusion mixed with a slight tone of concern enveloped the question as it timidly left Callie's lips.

"Yup. Mom loves to do the whole house tour. I bet she's been planning it since she found out you were coming."

A giggle that was laced with the tiniest bit of uncertainty sounded from Callie's throat as she allowed Jade to lead her into the cabin. And when they stepped over the threshold, Callie's mouth dropped open. Jade hadn't been exaggerating; this place looked like Christmas Central.

They were just taking their boots off at the front door, when the sound of little feet thundering on the linoleum floor of the hallway, touched Callie's ears. She glanced up to see two little girls, probably around six and eight running at top speed towards them.

"Auntie Jade!!" They both exclaimed in unison and Jade barely got her arms out in time to keep them from jumping onto her and knocking her over. Luckily, she managed to envelope them both in a bear hug instead.

"Girls! I've missed you. Where's Jordie?" Callie watched as Jade lifted her head upwards. Callie's gaze followed and within seconds, a tall, gangly teenage boy came strolling down the hallway. "Hey Jordie!"

"Hi Aunt Jade." Jordie's voice was high pitched and crackled as he spoke. Callie had to bite her lip to keep herself from laughing and when she glanced at Jade, she could tell that Jade was doing the same.

"Guys, I want you to meet my friend, Callie. Callie this is my nephew Jordan and my nieces, Lara and Britney."

"Hi!" Both the girls greeted her with enthusiasm but Jordan simply waved before turning around and heading back in the direction he had come from, with the girls skipping off right behind him.
After the children left, Jade started strolling down the hallway towards the back of the cabin, talking over her shoulder as she did. "Jordan, Lara and Britney are my sister, Tasha's kids. My brother, Landon has a daughter as well but mom said that they won't be getting here until later this evening."

Callie nodded as she listened and followed close behind Jade; her eyes moving back and forth as she surveyed her surroundings. Jade and Elliott had been right, the inside of the cabin, definitely had the log cabin feel, with wood furnishings and earthy tones, all of which were covered in tasteful Christmas decor. When they made their way to the end of the hallway, they entered the kitchen, which was bright due to the floor to ceiling windows on one wall and the French doors leading outside on the other. The appliances looked modern but the giant wood table and wooden bench seats, placed beside the glass sliding doors, helped to maintain the log cabin feel. As they entered the room, Jade's mom Courtney, a petite woman, with silver streaks in her dark hair and sparkling dark brown eyes stood up from her place at the kitchen table.

"Jade, sweetheart. I'm glad you made it safe."

Jade smiled warmly at her mother, who was quick to wrap Jade in her arms. "We always do mom." Courtney's mouth curved upwards. Then, as she stepped out of Jade's embrace, Courtney focused her eyes on Callie. "So good to see you again, Callie."

Callie smiled shyly while extending her hand out. "You too, Courtney."

Courtney glanced at Callie's hand but instead of shaking it, she threw her arms around Callie's shoulders. "In this house, my dear, we hug. Welcome, Callie. We're so glad you could join us."

Startled, Callie giggled nervously before placing her arms lightly around Courtney's back. After a moment, Courtney pulled away, and focused her eyes on the hallway. "Where's Elliott?"

Jade was pulling her jacket off when she answered. "He's grabbing our bags with dad."

Courtney nodded and then focused her attention back on Callie. "Let me show you to your room dear and then I can give you the grand tour."

Callie nodded and watched as Jade grinned widely and rolled her eyes. Jade's actions prompted a giggle to form in Callie's throat but she bit her lip to keep it from escaping her lips.

"Okay, mom, while you do that, I'll go find Tasha and Mike. Where are they?"

"Out back, collecting pine cones for the centrepieces. I asked the girls to do it but your sister insisted." Leaning close to Jade and Callie, Courtney spoke in a soft whisper. "I think she needed a break from the girls, they've been a little excited since they got here last night. Could barely get them to sleep last night." Laughter shook Jade's shoulders and Callie grinned widely at Courtney's confession.

"I can imagine." Jade grabbed her coat and shrugged her arms back into it. "I'll go help them." She then focused her gaze on her mother. "Go easy on Callie, mom. She's never had a big family Christmas before."

At Jade's comment, Courtney focused her gaze on Callie, her eyes wide with questions. "Really? Is that true?"

Callie nodded, as embarrassment shadowed her eyes. "Yes, ma'am. Growing up it was just me and my grandparents and when my grams passed, it was just me and Pops."

Callie watched as a wave of sympathy filled Courtney's eyes. "I'm sorry dear."

Callie shook her head while curving the corners of her mouth upwards. "It's okay. I had a good childhood. And I never had a big Christmas so I didn't know what I was missing, so I never really missed it, you know?"

Courtney's lips curled upwards and she nodded, a twinkle shining in her eyes. "That's very true, dear. But I'm glad you're here now."

Callie nodded as her light brown eyes sparkled brightly down at Courtney. "Me too."

Courtney kept her gaze locked on Callie for a moment; her lips still curled into a happy grin. After a few moments, she placed her hand on Callie's back and guided her out of the kitchen to begin the grand tour. When they were done, twenty minutes later, Callie was overwhelmed. There were eight bedrooms, each with their own bathroom, a living room, three other full bathrooms, a play room, a family room with the largest TV Callie had ever seen, and the massive kitchen. When they entered the living room at the end of the tour, Callie's eyes were bulging and the moment Jade's eyes landed on her, her shoulders shook with laughter.

"Mom, I told you to go easy on her."

Courtney glanced with wide, surprised eyes, from Jade to Callie and then back to Jade, clearly startled by Jade's comment. "I did." Courtney then turned her gaze back on Callie. "I'm sorry, Callie. I…"

Callie shook her head and offered Courtney a reassuring smile. "It's okay, Courtney. You were great. I'm just in awe of your house. It's amazing!"

Pride filled Courtney's eyes at Callie's compliment. "Thank you. It's always been a work in progress. It started out as a three bedroom and we've slowly added on through the years." Callie could hear the pride in Courtney's voice but before she could say anything else, loud voices interrupted them as Elliott, Nick and two people, whom Callie assumed were Tasha and her husband entered the living room.

Jade jumped up from her seat the moment the group appeared. "Callie, this is my sister Tasha and her husband Mike."

Callie's lips curled into a polite smile as she addressed Jade's sister and brother-in-law. "It's nice to meet you, both."

"You too, Callie." Tasha's dark brown eyes sparkled as she grinned brightly, revealing a set of perfectly white teeth. Tasha, like Jade was dressed impeccably. Her dark jeans and red sweater, looked like a designer brand and Callie was starting to feel her insecurity return until she turned her gaze on Mike.

Mike was a big man, with broad shoulders and a bit of a beer belly. He was bald, with a salt and pepper moustache and goatee. He was dressed in a pair of track pants and a white t-shirt, a complete contrast to his impeccable wife. He grinned at Callie as he addressed her. "Jade tells us that you're a mechanic at the dealership."

Callie nodded, grinning widely. "Yup. That's where we met."

Mike and Nick both looked impressed but before the conversation could continue, the loud bang of the front door crashing open prompted all eyes to turn towards the foyer. As they all stood in silence waiting, a smiling, dark blond, pig-tailed girl came rushing into the room. The girl's dark gray eyes found Courtney immediately and she leapt right into Courtney's arms. "Nana!!!"

Surprise filled Courtney's eyes as she wrapped her arms around the young girl. "Scar bear, what are you doing here? I thought you weren't going to be in until late tonight?"

"Daddy got off early so we got to come up early." The young girl looked around the room until her eyes landed on Nick. "Pops!"

The moment the little girl used the name Pops, Callie felt like she had been punched in the gut. It took everything in her to keep herself standing upright as she watched Nick envelope his grand-daughter in his arms. "Hey Scarlet. My little munchkin. Where's your dad?"

Pulling out of her grandfathers' arms, Scarlet turned her eyes towards the front door. "He's getting everything out of the car."

At that, both Elliott and Mike headed outside to help Scarlet's father. Callie was standing quietly in the corner of the room, trying to catch her breath when Scarlet narrowed her eyes on her. "Who are you?"

Everyone around her, smiled and giggled and Callie smiled brightly while bending down so that she was at eye level with the young girl. "I'm Callie. I'm a friend of your Aunt Jade's." Callie then stood up again and extended her hand towards Scarlet. "It's a pleasure to meet you."

Scarlet offered Callie a wide grin and Callie immediately noticed a dimple form on her left cheek and a cluster of red freckles that dotted her cheeks and nose. Scarlet grabbed Callie's hand and shook it wildly. "It's a pleasure to meet you too, Miss Callie." Everyone, including Callie smiled at Scarlet's polite, almost professional tone.

Callie opened her mouth to reply but before she could, Elliott and Mike came bustling back into the house, their arms full of bags and presents followed by a third man. As soon as Callie's eyes caught a glimpse of the third man, a gasp escaped her lips, prompting all eyes to focus on her. Callie's eyes widened in recognition and surprise and as she gasped, the man's eyes met hers and she could see them flash with recognition. His recognition quickly turned to surprise prompting him to stop abruptly.

"Miss Anderson?" Disbelief enveloped his words.

"Officer Pierce? What???"

"Why are you???"

They spoke in unison as everyone around them stared in silence. After a moment, Jade glanced from the man to Callie, then back to the man. "Officer Pierce? Landon what did you do?"

Jade's question prompted Callie to turn her gaze towards her friend. "Landon? Wait…" Callie glanced with wide eyes from Jade to Officer Pierce. "You're Jade's brother?"

Officer Pierce nodded; the look of surprise still evident in his smoldering gray eyes. "Since the day she was born and disrupted my happy life." There was a hint of teasing in his words and Jade smacked his arm before turning her focus to Callie.

"How do you two know each other? Since you know

him as Officer Pierce, I'm thinking it's not a good story." Without waiting for a response from Callie, Jade turned a dark, questioning gaze on her brother. "Landon, tell me you didn't do something stupid to my friend?"

Landon, who had his arms full of packages, stepped towards the corner of the room, dropped the packages down and then addressed his sister with slight annoyance ringing in his voice. "Jade, I'm the cop here. Why would you think that I was the one doing something stupid?"

"Because I know Callie and…"

Before Jade could continue, Callie stepped forwards, placing her hand on Jade's arm. "Actually, your brother is right. It was me. I, um…" She glanced around the room as all eyes focused on her and suddenly embarrassment began to creep up within her and she felt her cheeks flush. "Well, um, your brother was called to the bar when I punched someone." Callie's eyes immediately sought the ground and her shoulders slumped slightly, as gasps sounded from the group around her and Jade spoke with shock evident in her voice.

"You punched someone? How am I just hearing about this now?" As the question left her lips, Jade glanced down at Callie's right hand. She grabbed it and lifted it up, examining it as she did. "Wait. Is that how you got the bruises? I assumed it was a work thing."

Callie lifted her eyes up and stared at her friend. "Yeah. I, well, in my defense, the guy grabbed my backside twice and I told him if he did it again, I'd knock him out. He didn't believe me."

A whistle sounded from Elliott, and Mike laughed loudly. "Good for you." Mike's voice was filled with laughter

Tasha immediately smacked Mike across his chest. "Mike..."

Mike turned his eyes to his wife and shrugged his shoulders. "What? It's not like she didn't warn him. He was clearly harassing her."

Callie offered Mike a grateful smile and then turned her eyes to Tasha. "He was but I still shouldn't have..."

Before Callie could finish, Landon's voice sounded from beside her. "Hey. You had every right to defend yourself."

Callie turned her eyes to Landon and a flutter danced across her heart as she locked onto his beautiful gray eyes. "Thanks, but..."

Before Callie could finish, Courtney spoke up. "So, what happened then, Landon? Did you have to arrest Callie?"

Landon shook his head but kept his eyes focused on Callie. "Not that time." Landon's voice was deep and enveloped in amusement as a twinkle danced in his eyes.

"Wait, what?" Jade's words came out in a high-pitched shriek.

"What do you mean 'not that time', son?" Nick spoke from his position beside Courtney and Callie could detect a hint of amusement in his voice. "Are you telling us that you and Callie have crossed paths on more than one occasion?"

Callie broke her eyes away from Landon and turned

them towards Nick as her cheeks began to burn and she suspected that they had turned a deep shade of red. "Well, yeah…there was another time."

"And you arrested her?" Jade was staring daggers at her brother but Landon had an amused grin touching his lips and the twinkle was still dancing in his eyes.

"No, I didn't actually arrest her, Jade." He turned his focus to his sister as he continued. "I was just playing. I did pull her over for speeding, though."

Callie turned her eyes back up to Landon. "And you very graciously let me go with just a warning."

Landon grinned down at her and Callie felt her heart flip flop in her chest as she thought that he was even more handsome in his civilian clothes. "But next time…"

"I know, you'll throw the book at me."

Everyone around her started to laugh and Landon winked and nodded his head. "That's right, Miss Anderson."

"Please, call me Callie."

Landon nodded but then tilted his head and raised an eyebrow. "Okay, Callie, but I'm confused. What are you doing in my family's cabin?"

Callie opened her mouth to answer but Jade stepped forward, linking her arm with Callie's and answering for her. "This is the friend I told you about, from work. She doesn't have any family so I invited her to spend the holidays with us."

Landon nodded again, but didn't respond. He just stared at Callie for a second before turning around and heading back outside. Callie stared after him before being pulled towards the kitchen by Jade and Courtney. As she followed the two women, she tried to focus on the conversation they were having but her mind was preoccupied with thoughts of Officer Pierce. The handsome, rugged, officer who had occupied her thoughts constantly since the day they had met and the officer whom she thought she would never see again but was suddenly in her orbit once again.

Chapter 5

Landon stared at Callie in silence. His heart was racing as her soft, pink lips curled into the beautiful smile that had occupied his every thought for days. After a moment, he cleared his throat and, then turned around quickly, feeling the sudden need to escape the room. Dashing back to the snowy world outside, he made a beeline for his SUV and as he was rummaging around with the last few suitcases in the trunk, he was so distracted that he jumped and his heart slammed against his chest when his father's voice rang out through the crisp, winter air.

"That was an interesting story."

"What?" Whipping around, Landon's hand landed on his chest as his wide, surprised eyes focused on his father. "Jesus, dad. You just startled the shit out of me."

There was a twinkle in his father's eyes as a soft chuckle escaped his lips. "Sorry about that, son. That wasn't my intention."

Landon nodded, waiting to speak until the pounding of his heart subsided. "I know. Sorry, I just didn't hear you behind me."

"Distracted by something or *someone*?" His father's head tilted slightly as he lifted his eyebrow in question.

Landon scoffed at his father's emphasis on the last word, then rolled his eyes while shaking his head. "No, dad. It's just been a long week and I'm tired."

His father nodded but didn't say anything else. Instead, he grabbed the last bag out of Landon's trunk, but the moment Landon slammed the trunk door closed a little harder than necessary, his father tilted his head again. "Things okay with you?"

A small sigh left Landon's throat. "Yeah, I'm fine dad. It's just been busy. It's the season, things get a little hectic down at the station."

His father offered him a slight smile and the twinkle of mischief dancing in his eyes did not escape Landon's notice. "With women punching men and speeding…"

"Dad…." A tone of annoyance clung to Landon's words as he shot his father a look of warning.

His father grinned widely, holding up his free hand in surrender. "Okay. I'm sorry. It's just, I noticed that you and Callie seemed to…"

"Seemed to what?" Landon's tone was short as he cut his father off mid-sentence.

A twinkle shone in his father's eyes as he shook his head. "Nothing. Forget I said anything, son. Shall we get inside? I think your mother has lunch almost ready, I'm starving."

Landon nodded and then followed as his father led the way into the cabin. As they walked, Landon's mind wandered back to Callie; the woman whom he thought he would never see again but kept reappearing in his world. And

44

every time she did, he felt a wave of happiness mixed with nervous energy course through his body; two feelings that he hadn't experienced in a very long time. And both those feelings enveloped Landon throughout the day as he got himself and Scarlet settled in their rooms.

When he arrived at the table for dinner that evening, he was pleased but not surprised to see that his mother had placed him and Callie side by side. As he sat down, and glanced at the feast in front of him, he felt butterflies dance in his stomach when his eyes landed on her. Her eyes were wide as she surveyed the table in front of her and he watched as she closed her eyes and took a deep breath in. As a smile touched her lips, a small smile began to form across his own lips and as the large group began to pass the various, colourful dishes around the table, curiosity about her and why she was here with his family began to envelope him.

Chapter 6

As she sat in her seat at the dinner table that night, Callie's eyes widened as she glanced around at the wide variety of colourful food selections displayed in fancy dishes on the festively decorated table in front of her. She took a deep breath, closing her eyes in an effort to focus her senses solely on the delicious smells wafting through the air around her. When she re-opened her eyes, she was immediately aware of Landon's presence beside her and as everyone began dishing food onto their Santa Claus dinner plates, she could sense him watching her. She was also very aware of his knee brushing up against hers whenever he moved to pass one of the dishes around the table and the heat from his knee radiating through her, created goosebumps all over her body. As she listened to the lively conversations happening around her, she was trying to think of something interesting to say to him, but before anything smart popped into her mind, she felt him lean in and the sound of his voice danced into her ears.

"I think my mom may have gone a little overboard."

Callie lifted her eyes up and when her gaze rested on his twinkling eyes, a flutter of excitement danced across her chest. Curling her lips, she glanced around the table before responding to give herself time to think, so that she didn't say anything stupid. When her eyes landed back on him, he was grinning down at her, his dark, sparkling eyes shining brightly.

She returned his smile. "Yeah, and I can't wait to try every dish."

Laughter danced in his eyes. "Neither can I. But I have to warn you, Callie, after this trip you may have to buy a whole new wardrobe." His grin widened and laughter shook her shoulders as they continued to load his mother's delicious meal onto their plates.

Callie ate in silence after that, content to soak up the fun and laughter from the family around her and as she was finishing her meal, she felt Landon lean close to her once again.

"So, Callie, isn't your family going to miss you for Christmas?"

Bringing her eyes up to his as her name left his lips, she quickly diverted them downwards as his question touched her ears. As she focused on the plate in front of her, she could feel his eyes lingering on her, waiting for a response. "Um, well…" She lifted her eyes back up to meet his and swallowed hard, before continuing with soft, quiet words. "Actually, it's just me."

His eyes widened in surprise. "Oh, Callie, I'm sorry. I didn't realize." Apology surrounded his words and crept into the corners of his eyes.

She shook her head and offered him a reassuring smile. "It's okay, Landon. How could you?" He nodded and then quickly turned his attention back to his plate as an awkward silence enveloped them.

A few minutes later, wanting to escape the awkwardness, Callie stood up and began clearing the table as everyone around her continued their lively conversations. As she carried a stack of plates into the kitchen, she found herself face to face with Landon, who was loading the dishwasher and had clearly had the same idea as her. "Hey." Her voice was louder than she had anticipated, and she immediately felt heat warming her cheeks.

He flashed her a wide grin. "Hey."

Silence surrounded them again as they both turned their attention to the dirty dishes around them. After a few minutes, Landon cleared his throat, prompting Callie to turn her gaze up to meet his, as he spoke softly. "I'm sorry about earlier, I didn't mean to…"

She quickly shook her head. "No, it's all good Landon. You don't have to apologize. I'm the one that made it awkward."

Straightening from his position at the dishwasher, Landon raised his eyebrows and stared at her with confusion dancing in his eyes. "How did you make it awkward?"

Offering him a sheepish grin, she shrugged her shoulders. "Well, I just kind of blurted that information out."

Landon shook his head as he went back to stacking dishes in the machine, keeping his eyes focused on her the entire time. "I wouldn't say that. You were just answering my question. I made it awkward by being so intrusive. I'm sorry about that. I was just curious." Callie nodded but didn't respond and her silence allowed Landon to continue. "And I still am, if you want to talk about it."

A faint smile touched the corners of her mouth. "There isn't much to say, really." Leaning against the counter behind her, she crossed her arms, and focused her eyes on him. "My mom passed away when I was three and I was raised by my grandparents until my grams died when I was seven, after that it was just me and Pops."

"And where is your Pops now? Does he not still live

in town?" His question was soft but enveloped in curiosity.

Callie shook her head as a flash of sadness crossed her eyes and a pang of pain stabbed her heart. "He passed away seven years ago."

Landon's eyes grew wide, and a pink hue crept onto his cheeks. "Callie, I'm sorry, I should have assumed that. I didn't mean to be so insensitive."

Shaking her head again, her eyes remained cloaked in sadness but her lips curled into a reassuring smile. "It's okay Landon."

Eyeing her with apology filled eyes, he shook his head. "No, it's not." He turned his back to her to grab more dishes, while still shaking his head and when he turned to look at her again, she could see that the pink hue had turned a dark shade of red. "I'm an idiot. I talk too much."

Callie reached over and placed her hand gently on his arm. "You aren't an idiot, Landon. A stranger has just invaded your family Christmas, I think it's okay to be curious." Her voice was gentle and the sadness in her eyes faded as they filled with warmth.

Landon's lips curled upwards and he stepped back to lean against the counter using his hands as support behind him. His eyes sparkled as he shook his head. "Curious yes, but not insensitive and intrusive."

His description of himself elicited a giggle to escape her throat. "You weren't being either of those things, trust me. And to be honest, I don't mind talking about Pops." She smiled but the moment those words were out of her mouth, a wave of unexpected sadness washed over her as memories of her Pops flashed through her mind. Her eyes misted over and the moment they did, she noticed a worried crease spread across Landon's forehead.

"Are you okay?" His voice was dripping with concern.

Smiling at both the memory of her Pops and the sweet concern in Landon's voice, Callie nodded. "I am. I just miss him."

Landon nodded; the concern in his eyes was now mixed with a flicker of sadness. "I get that. It's how I feel about Izzie. My wife, she passed…"

Callie nodded; her eyes filling with sympathy. "Jade told me. I'm so sorry Landon."

Shaking his head quickly, the sadness in Landon's eyes vanished as he turned his attention to the sink full of dishes. "Sorry, I didn't mean to make that about me."

"Landon, you didn't. I understand." Her voice was soft as he turned his gaze back to her. She smiled and they held each other's focus for a moment before they both turned away. Staring down at the dishes, Callie grabbed the tea towel that was sitting beside the sink. "You wash and I'll dry?"

A wide grin broke out across Landon's features. "Do that and you will be my mother's favourite all week."

Callie straightened her shoulders and turned her smile into a serious gaze. "Well, in that case, we'd better get started." Her attempt at being serious broke when Landon began to laugh. Within seconds, Callie was laughing with him and then they began their chore giggling as they did. As they stood side by side, working, Callie felt Landon's eyes on her, so she

51

glanced up and found him eying her with curiosity.

"Will you tell me about your Pops? I mean, if you want to. I don't want to make you sad again, but you did mention that you don't mind talking about him and well, I'd like to hear about him if you want to tell me." The words rushed out of his mouth and nervous energy surrounded his body, prompting Callie's lips to curl upwards. A giggle passed through her lips, causing him to raise his eyebrows. "What's so funny?"

She shook her head, still giggling softly. "Nothing, really. It's just, you seem so different tonight, than you did the first couple times our paths crossed. That serious, but fair, police man has been replaced by a…"

Landon stopped what he was doing and focused all his attention on her. "A, what?" Curiosity surrounded his question.

"A charming school boy."

Landon's eyes widened. "Did you just call me a charming school boy?"

She giggled, feeling heat rising in her cheeks. "Yeah, but I meant it in a good way. Sorry, I can't always find the right words. I just meant, you're softer…"

"Softer?" He raised an eyebrow above his sparkling, gray eyes.

"No, yes…" Her uncertainty prompted amusement to dance in his eyes, as she continued to try to explain herself. "I just mean. You were kind to me before, but you had this persona going on, I mean, like you were doing a job, but here, you seem relaxed and happy."

Landon's lips curled upwards but he didn't speak, he just continued to stare at her. Her eyes latched onto his, and as she was getting lost in his smoldering gray eyes, she felt a splash of water hit her cheeks.

"What the?" She placed her hands in front of her face to stop the water attack and as she did, she noticed Landon's eyes twinkling with mischief. His lips turned upwards into a wide, mischievous grin. "Lan…" Before she could finish her sentence, another splash of water hit her face and before she knew it, her hands were in the sink splashing water in his direction. As the water soaked their clothes, and their laughter filled the kitchen, a voice behind them made them both freeze in their tracks.

"What is going on in here?"

At the sound of Courtney's voice, Callie's back straightened. She glanced briefly at Landon, who had also straightened up. They giggled quietly before turning around to face Courtney.

"Mom, hey!" Landon's voice was as casual as he could make it but Callie heard a hint of amusement lying beneath the surface.

Callie felt like a kid who had just been caught being naughty as she tried not to giggle. "Courtney, hi. We were just doing the dishes."

"Right. Yeah, mom. We thought it would be nice to…"

Courtney, who was watching them with laughter dancing in her eyes, interrupted; her tone was choked in amusement. "Splash water all over my kitchen floor…"

Callie's eyes moved from Courtney to Landon, whose gaze landed on her as well, and as soon as their eyes met, they both started shaking with laughter.

Courtney shook her head and rolled her eyes as Callie and Landon continued to laugh. "Okay, you two hooligans. I'm glad you're getting along and that no one is getting arrested but clean this up, please."

"Yes, mom." Landon stopped laughing long enough to answer her, but Callie could hear laughter lingering in his voice.

Courtney glanced from Landon to Callie, before shaking her head again and walking away, amusement still dancing in her eyes. When Courtney had disappeared from the room, the two of them went back to their task, side by side at the sink. They worked in silence for a while, and although she kept her eyes focused on the dishes, every once in a while, she could feel his eyes on her. She didn't speak or look back up at him until she heard him clear his throat.

"So, um, do you want to talk about your Pops?"

Turning her gaze up to him, she offered him a warm smile as the image of her grandfather filled her mind. "Do you really want to hear my boring life story?"

Landon's eyes narrowed on her, and they quickly softened as he nodded. "Of course. And I doubt I'll find it boring." The soft tone of his voice caused her knees to weaken, catching her by surprise. She leaned into the counter to prevent herself from falling and then, staring down at the sink, she took a moment to steady herself before glancing back up at him.

"Well, as I told you I was raised by my grandparents from the time I was three. My mom passed away and that just left me and my grandparents."

"What about your dad?"

Callie shook her head while turning her attention back to the dishes in front of her. She began drying them as she spoke. "I never knew him. My mom never told my grandparents who he was."

Feeling the warmth of Landon's hand touch her shoulder, she brought her eyes up to meet his gaze. "Callie, I'm sorry."

As the warmth of his touch flowed through her, she offered him a reassuring smile. "It's okay Landon. It's not your fault, and I made my peace with it a long time ago."

"You've never thought about doing one of those DNA tests?"

"Not really." She replied while shaking her head but as soon as those words left her lips, she rolled her eyes and offered him a sheepish smile. "Okay, well, that's not entirely true. I did think about it, right after I lost Pops. I was feeling alone and wondered if I had more family out there but..." Without finishing her thought, she dropped her head down, breaking eye contact with him.

"But…"

She drew her eyes up to meet his again, as she replied quietly. "But I didn't do it. I think I was too scared to find out. Does that make sense?"

He nodded and the look in his eyes implored her to continue. She took a deep breath but before she continued, she dropped the tea towel, turned around and leaned against the counter, using the counter for support as she prepared to tell him things, she had never told anyone.

"When grams died, I was young, but I still had Pops and he was the most amazing person. I don't remember my mom at all, and I only remember Grams vaguely. She was sick and in and out of the hospital for the last couple years of her life. So, I only really remember her in a hospital bed, hooked up to machines, but Pops, Pops was my whole world, and I was his." Her eyes drifted past Landon, as she focused on the window behind him. Nostalgia clouded her eyes as she thought about the man who had raised her. Her focus stayed on the outside world as she continued her story. "Even though he had raised my mom, he had Grams there, so he didn't have to worry too much about things but when I came along, suddenly here was this seventy-year-old man, in charge of a seven-year-old girl. But he never complained, he never made me feel like a burden. All I ever felt was his love and his pride." Her eyes drifted back to meet Landon's gaze and he was regarding her with gentle eyes and a warm smile stretched across his lips. Callie felt a feeling of safety surrounding him and she felt herself relax as she continued her story. "He was a mechanic and would take me to the shop after school every day. And he would teach me things and let me help him." A happy smile touched her eyes as she embraced her memories. "I still remember being this seven-year-old kid, with messy pigtails and a gap-toothed grin passing him tools as he laid under a car. It was the best. I miss it." Her last three words were edged in sadness, but a smile was etched across her lips as she continued. "But I also remember that even though we spent most of our time covered in grease and dirt, Pops made sure that I still got to be a little girl. He bought me barbies and played with me, and we had tea parties."

Landon smiled widely at that. "He sounds like an amazing man, Callie."

Feeling an overwhelming sense of love as she thought about her grandfather, Callie felt tears welling in her eyes, prompting her to bend her head and stare down at her feet. Her voice was quiet when she responded. "He was."

Silence surrounded them after that and after a few seconds, Callie turned around and put her focus back on the dishes in the sink. Landon followed suit and they worked side by side in silence.

When the last dish was put away, Landon picked up his glass of wine and leaned against the counter across from her, crossing his ankles and staring at her with appreciation flowing through his dark gray eyes. "Thank you for sharing that with me."

Callie grabbed her own glass of wine and touched it to her lips. She sipped slowly, taking the moment to compose her thoughts. "Thank you for listening. I've never said any of that out loud to another person before." Holding his eyes with hers, she offered him a soft smile. "You're easy to talk to." He opened his mouth to respond but the corners of her mouth turned upwards into a smirk and a twinkle danced in her eyes as she continued, stopping his response before it started. "Which is surprising since you've already tried to arrest me, twice."

A surprise gasp escaped his lips but almost immediately laughter began to dance in his eyes. "Well, I'm not sure I'd agree with that assessment. The arresting part, I mean. I do agree that I'm a good listener."

The twinkle in her eyes remained but the amusement left her lips and was replaced with a grateful smile. "You are and I'm grateful."

Landon nodded slightly, offering her a warm smile as they stood across from each other, sipping their wine. The silence between them was comfortable and Callie felt a wave of happiness flow through her. She was thinking about how happy she was that she was standing here in this kitchen, when the swinging door flew open and Scarlet came barreling into the room.

"Daddy, Nana told me to tell you and Callie that the

movie starts in ten minutes." Landon nodded and Scarlet turned around but then stopped abruptly. Turning back towards them, she glanced from her father to Callie and then back to her father. "Oh, and she also told me to tell you that the kitchen better be spotless!"

Callie let out a loud laugh, prompting Scarlet's facial features to scrunch up in confusion but she didn't ask the question on her mind, instead, she just turned back around and headed back out of the kitchen. Callie watched her go and then turned her gaze to Landon, who was shaking his head. "I think you got me into trouble."

Callie's mouth dropped open and she was about to protest when she saw a flicker of mischief dance in his eyes. Slapping him playfully across the arm, she rolled her eyes, and then responded with amusement enveloping her words. "And if you aren't nice to me, I'll do it again."

At her response laughter surrounded the room and then after taking one last look around the kitchen to ensure everything was tidy, they headed out to watch the movie with his family.

Chapter 7

After watching both 'Rudolph the Red Nosed Reindeer' and 'Frosty the Snowman', the children were ushered off to bed by their parents and Callie decided to use that opportunity to step outside for a little alone time. Bundled up in her warm winter coat, she grabbed herself a cup of hot cocoa from the kitchen and made her way out to the front porch. Sitting down on the middle of the two-person swing, she leaned back against the padded cushion and slowly pushed the swing with one of her feet. Taking a deep breath of the chilly, crisp mountain air, she gazed up into the night sky. As she enjoyed the quiet night and bright, twinkling stars above her, she didn't hear the door open, or the footsteps approaching her until a deep voice broke into her peace.

"Oh, I'm sorry, I didn't know anyone was out here." Startled, she jumped, spilling hot cocoa onto her lap. "Oh, sorry, Callie. I didn't..."

The corners of her mouth curved upwards as she stared up into Landon's apologetic eyes. As she wiped the mess from her jeans, she shook her head trying to reassure him. "It's all good, Landon. That's what washing machines are for."

Relief passed across his features as he gazed down at her, a smile touching the corners of his eyes. "True." He held her gaze for a moment, before turning his focus to the dark, clear, sky. "It sure is a beautiful night."

Callie's lips curled upwards as she returned her eyes up to the sky and breathed out a contented sigh. "It is. It's so peaceful out here."

A half laugh, half scoff escaped Landon's lips as he replied with sarcasm dripping from his words. "Yeah, out here, maybe. In there it's chaos."

Laughter immediately flew out of Callie's mouth and her eyes were dancing when she met his eyes with her own. "Is that why you came out here? To get away from the chaos."

"Isn't that why you're out here?"

"No! Of course not." Her denial was a little too fast and defensive, prompting him to raise an eyebrow and when he did, she offered him a slightly, sheepish grin. "Okay, maybe a little." She giggled and his mouth curved into a wide grin. "But in my defense, I'm not used to being around so many people. What's your excuse?"

"Oh, I just hate people. Especially those ones." Amusement enveloped his words and laughter shook Callie's shoulders as she quickly responded with a smirk touching her lips.

"I bet you do. They seem awful!"

"Oh, they are. Don't let their kind faces and sweet demeanors fool you." A smirk curved his lips as laughter flew out of Callie's mouth.

After a moment, when her laughter had died down, she scooted over and motioned to the empty cushion beside her. "Would you care to join me?"

His dark eyes sparkled against the back drop of the moonlight as he peered down at her, nodding as he did. "I'd love to."

"Anything to get away from the chaos, right?"

Her retort brought laughter to his eyes. "Oh, absolutely. I mean, I don't normally hang out with those who break the law."

Her mouth dropped open and she whipped her head towards him but the amusement in his eyes was contagious as a grin spread across her lips. "You are a funny man, Officer Pierce."

The sparkle in his eyes turned into a twinkle of mischief as he beamed down at her, clearly proud of himself. "Why thank you, Miss Anderson. I think so too."

Callie shook her head at his response but couldn't control the laughter that was dancing in her eyes. They grinned at each other, before returning their attentions back to the beautiful night above them. Silence surrounded them for several moments, until Callie heard a sigh slip out of Landon's mouth. She turned her eyes towards him and noticed that the laughter had left his features. His voice was quiet and he kept his gaze upwards when he began to speak. "Izzie used to love it up here. Christmas was her favourite time of year."

Callie nodded, watching him. His eyes had softened and the smile touching his lips held a hint of nostalgia.

"Would you tell me about her?"

He slowly turned his eyes on her. "Iz?"

She nodded, smiling softly. "If you want to. I'd like to hear about her but I don't want to intrude."

Landon didn't speak as his eyes moistened and Callie saw tears puddle in the corners of them, which caused regret to hover within her. But within seconds Landon's lips curled upwards and Callie watched as nostalgia and joy flickered in his eyes. "You aren't intruding." He paused and Callie continued watching him as he turned his eyes back up to the stars above them. He started to move so that the swing swayed beneath them and she curled her legs up underneath her, enjoying the ride. After a moment he turned his gaze back to her. There was sadness gathering in the corners of his eyes, but when he spoke a smile touched his lips. "Izzie was the light of my life. She was beautiful and kind and funny and she had the most amazing laugh. She lit up the world around her and she was so strong."

The corners of Callie's mouth curved upwards at the love that enveloped his words and she could see the love he had for his wife reflecting in his eyes. "How did you meet?"

Her question elicited instant laughter to ooze out of him. "Actually, I almost arrested her."

Callie snorted, prompting Landon to laugh even louder. She covered her mouth as heat touched her cheeks. Their eyes locked for a moment until Callie's embarrassment subsided enough for her to speak. "What did she do?"

Landon shook his head as memory twinkled in his eyes. "Well, she was at a bar for her sister's bachelorette party and she got into a bit of an argument with a guy who didn't know the rules of European football."

Callie laughed as her eyes grew wide. "You're kidding?"

Landon grinned while shaking his head. "Nope. My girl was really into sports and she didn't like to be told she was wrong."

Callie shook her head as laughter sounded from her lips. "Wow. I think I like her."

As Landon locked his eyes onto hers, his eyes softened but his lips remained curled upwards. "Yeah, I think you would have and she would have liked you too. The two of you have the same spirit."

Amusement danced in Callie's eyes. "Why do you say that? Is it because the first time you met me; I had also just gotten into an argument at a bar?" There was a hint of mischief in her voice, prompting Landon to chuckle softly.

His dark gray eyes sparkled when he answered. "Maybe." A smirk then formed slowly across his lips. "But at least Izzie didn't punch anyone. She just broke a couple glasses."

Callie tried her best to look innocent but the recollection of that night in the bar prompted laughter to escape her lips. "True. But in my defense, that guy had it coming. I warned him."

Landon's shoulders shook with laughter. "I remember."

Their eyes held as they laughed but Landon quickly broke eye contact prompting Callie to stop laughing, and clear her throat. "Okay, so enough about that. Tell me more. How did you go from almost arresting her to marrying her?"

Silence washed over him then and Callie noticed a cloud of mist enter his eyes. He stared absently, off into the dark night for a moment before answering; his gaze remaining on the night when he spoke. "Well, after the owner of the bar agreed not to charge her if she paid for the damages, I let her go. When she was walking away with her friends, she turned back, pulled a card out of her pocket, and handed it to me. I didn't look down at it, I was too mesmerized by her to see anything but her and just before she disappeared around the corner, she glanced over her shoulder, smiled and then winked." He paused, then and turned his gaze on Callie. "At that moment, I swear I stopped breathing, she literally took my breath away. When I looked down at the card, I saw that it was her business card, she owned a little flower shop downtown. Her cell number was on it and…" He paused for another moment, letting out a long deep breath. "And after that I was hooked. I called her the next day and we got married a year to the day that we met, we even had our engagement party at that bar."

Callie's eyes twinkled as she grinned, feeling the warmth of his love for his wife envelope them both. "That's a pretty great story. Izzie sounds amazing."

Landon sighed as the sadness returned to his eyes. "She was."

"You must miss her a lot."

His head bobbed up and down slowly. "I do. But it's been four years and everyone thinks that I should have moved on by now, but it's not that easy. I mean, I know that they just want me to be happy but Izzie was my wife and I just…" Callie could hear tears enveloping his words. She instinctively reached over and touched his arm and the moment their skin connected, his eyes snapped to her hands on him and he cleared his throat. When he looked back into her eyes, Callie saw a mix of embarrassment and apology swimming in his eyes. "I'm sorry. That was…"

Callie removed her hand from his arm and offered

him an encouraging smile. "It was honest. Thank you for sharing."

His smiled weakly and nodded his head but didn't speak. Instead, he leaned back in the swing and let his eyes roam back up to the sky. Callie watched him for a moment and then followed his lead, wrapping her jacket a little tighter around her shoulders, as the chill of the night touched her skin. As they sat in silence, Callie peeked over at him; his eyes were focused on the stars twinkling in the sky above. She watched him for a moment, before turning her own eyes up to watch the twinkling lights. And as she did, she thought of the memories they had shared and felt a wave of amazement wash over her. Here at this cabin, talking to this stranger was the most comfortable she had been with someone in a long time. And as they continued to sit together in silence, she let the comfort she was feeling with him beside her, wrap itself around her.

Chapter 8

Landon crawled out from his comfy, king-sized bed after his first night at the cabin, way before the sun was due to peak out through the dawn. Sleep had eluded him for most of the night and when he did manage to find rest, both Izzie and Callie had invaded his dreams. And now as he watched the first signs of daylight climbing over the mountain from his perch on the porch swing, a feeling of restlessness coursed through his body. As the swing moved slowly underneath him, his thoughts wandered back to the night before when he and Callie were sitting on this very swing, talking about Izzie. It wasn't often that he spoke about his late wife and when he did it was never with someone he had just met. But there was something about Callie that made him feel comfortable, like they were old friends, and made him want to confide in her. He felt an easiness talking to her that he hadn't felt with anyone in a long time. "Not since Izzie." He confessed quietly to the silent morning.

"Not since Izzie, what?"

At the sound of Callie's soft voice, Landon jumped in his seat as his heart thumped against his chest. Jerking his head up in the direction of her voice, he placed his hand over his chest. "Jesus!"

A sheepish grin inched across her lips as she looked down on him with apologetic eyes. "Sorry, Landon. I didn't mean to..." Her voice trailed off as he stared up at her.

After letting out a calming breath, he lowered his hand and nodded. "I know." Offering her a reassuring smile, he motioned to the empty cushion beside him. "It's all good. Care to join me?"

He watched as a flicker of uncertainty danced in her eyes but it was quickly replaced with a sparkle as a smile touched her lips. "Sure. I'd like that. I love this swing. I think it may be my favourite part of the house."

Landon grinned and his eyes followed her movements as she sat down beside him. "Mine too." He replied as their eyes locked. After a moment, he broke his eyes away and swept them across the snow-covered trees in front of him. "I love it out here. It's so serene."

"It is!" Enthusiasm enveloped her words, which prompted Landon's lips to curl upwards as he continued to survey the scenery around him. It had snowed overnight, so there was a fresh layer of fluffy, white snow covering the front yard and the trees were sparkling, as the rays of the early morning sun began to touch them. The scene before him was picturesque and as he leaned back against the swing, he inhaled deeply, allowing the scent of pine needles and fresh snow to fill his lungs. Hearing Callie breath deeply as well, prompted another smile to touch his lips.

They sat together in silence for a while, enjoying the serenity of the morning, and just as he felt Callie shift in her seat like she was about to say something, the front door opened abruptly. Turning, he was greeted with the surprised but smiling face of his father.

"Hey you two!" Surprise enveloped his father's words. "I didn't think anyone else was up yet."

Landon's lips curled upwards and noting how warmly his dad was dressed, he raised an eyebrow in question. "Where are you headed so early, dad?"

His father grinned as a twinkle glimmered in his

eyes. "You know your mother. She's already planning dinner and she needs a few things from the store. Wanted me to go before breakfast."

Landon's shoulders shook as he imagined the conversation that had probably preceded this moment. "Yeah, that sounds about right. Do you want some company?"

His father grinned down at him, allowing his twinkling eyes to move from him to Callie and then back to him. "No, thanks son. You stay here and enjoy the company." Landon detected a hint of amusement in his dad's voice and he immediately felt heat flooding his cheeks. He knew his father must have seen it as well because he quickly cleared his throat before turning his gaze to the snowy landscape in front of them. "And the view too!"

Landon rolled his eyes and tried not to laugh at his father's awkward attempt to cover. Silence surrounded the three of them until Callie shifted in her seat and cleared her throat.

"Landon and I were just watching the sunrise and it's quite a view, Nick. It must be wonderful to have such an amazing place to spend time at."

The corners of Landon's mouth curved upwards, knowing that Callie had just struck the right chord with his father. Glancing from her to his father, Landon watched his father's face fill with pride as he straightened his shoulders and grinned widely down at her. "Yes, it is Callie. And it's even better having our whole family with us, especially at Christmas. And we're delighted to have you with us this year too, young lady."

Landon scoffed at that and immediately felt Callie's

hand hit his jacket protected arm.

"What was that, mister?"

Turning his gaze to her, he offered her his most innocent smile. "Nothing. I didn't say anything."

Callie rolled her eyes and his father laughed while stepping towards the stairs. "Well, I think I'll leave you two, to it. I have groceries to buy." He ambled down the stairs, waving to them as he went. "I'll see you both later."

"See you dad."

"Bye Nick. Drive safe."

The two of them watched in silence as his father hit the ground at the bottom of the stairs and then turn back towards them. "I will. And son?"

Landon tilted his head, curiosity filling his eyes.

"Behave yourself, will you?"

Landon's eyes widened and his mouth gaped open, completely caught off guard by his father's words. As he was trying to think of a response, he heard the sound of Callie's laughter beside him. Turning his gaze, he aimed questioning eyes on her. "And just what are you laughing at, missy?"

She shook her head while laughter continued to shake her shoulders. After taking a moment to compose herself, she raised her hands up in mock surrender. "Nothing, nothing at all Officer." Amusement framed her words, prompting Landon to roll his eyes.

"Yeah right." His response dripped with sarcasm.

They grinned at each other then and then he heard the sound of his father's laughter; drawing Landon's attention away from Callie. "Try to get along, you two." His dad's words were fueled with amusement as they left his lips but he didn't stick around to hear a response. Instead, he strolled down the path towards his car as both Landon and Callie stared after him.

"My dad is a funny man."

Callie snorted as she shook with laughter. "Agreed."

Raising his eyebrows in her direction, Landon tilted his head. "You think it's funny, do you?" His words were laced with quiet amusement.

Her eyes were dancing as she nodded. "A little. I mean, how often do you hear a grown man being scolded by his father."

Exasperation framed Landon's face and he tried to stare at her with annoyed eyes but even he could see the humour in the situation and his annoyance quickly turned to amusement. They were both shaking with laughter when his father came hustling back up the walkway.

"Okay, you two jokers, enough laughing. I need some help."

Landon, immediately, turned his focus to his father. "Dad, I thought you were going to the store?"

His father scoffed. "Yeah, me too." He rubbed the back of his neck while glancing from Landon to Callie and then back to Landon. "Stupid car won't start. It's probably the battery. Want to give me a boost?"

Before Landon could respond, Callie jumped up from her seat, startling him as she did. Her voice was cloaked in excitement as she stared down at his father. "Can I take a look at it, Nick? Just to make sure that's what the problem is?"

His father quickly shook his head. "No, Callie. Thank you, but I couldn't ask you to…"

Holding up her hand and shaking her own head, Callie stopped him mid-sentence. "It's the least I can do. And I want to."

His father stared at her for a moment before breaking out into a wide grin. He shook his head and used his hand to motion her towards his car. "All righty, if you insist, be my guest."

As soon as the words were out of his mouth, Callie bounced down the stairs, sporting a wide, happy grin. "I do." She replied with a giggle as she rushed past him, leaving both him and Landon staring at her as she skipped towards the driveway.

His dad then turned his attention to him. "Well, I don't think I've ever seen anyone so excited about a dead battery." Laughter framed his words and Landon chuckled, while nodding his head in agreement.

"Me neither." Standing up, Landon quickly descended the stairs and marched towards his father. "Come on, let's go see what all the excitement is about, shall we?"

His father laughed and then quickly followed as Landon passed him and headed towards the drive way. When they got to the car, the hood was already up and all they could see of Callie was her backside as she leaned into the car. Landon tried to avert his eyes but the tight jeans she was wearing, showed off the perfect curves of her body and he couldn't keep himself from staring.

As they approached her, Callie popped her head out from under the hood and focused her eyes on his father. "Can you try starting it for me, Nick? So, I can see what we're dealing with."

His dad nodded and then shuffled to the driver's door, lowering himself into the front seat. As he did, Callie turned her attention back to the engine. Within seconds, she turned sparkling eyes on Landon; a wide smile lighting up her whole face. "That's what I thought, it's the starter."

As his father climbed out of the car both Landon and Callie diverted their eyes towards him and Callie quickly filled him in on her assessment. "It's the starter."

Sighing loudly, he bowed his head in defeat but Callie's cheerful voice quickly broke through his solemness.

"I can fix it in like an hour. All I need are the parts. Is there a garage on the mountain?"

Both men shook their heads but it was Landon who responded. "No. We'd have to go back into the city.

Callie glanced from Landon to his father and then back to Landon as the sparkle in her eyes shone brightly. "Well, I don't know about you Officer, but I don't have anywhere to be today."

Before Landon could reply, he heard a scoff echo from beside him prompting him to turn his attention to his father. "Callie, I couldn't ask you to do that. It'll take three hours to get to town and back and then by the time you get it all fixed, it'll eat up your whole day."

Callie shook her head and shrugged her shoulders and was about to reply but Landon spoke up before her, focusing his eyes on her. "I don't mind, Callie, if you don't. I wouldn't mind picking up a few things in town and we can get the groceries for mom."

Callie's smile grew and the sparkle touching her eyes turned to excitement. "I don't mind at all." She was buzzing with excitement as she turned her attention back to his father, who shrugged while shaking his head and smiling at them both.

"Well, if you don't mind spending your vacation working, Callie, then alright."

"It's the least I can do Nick. And besides, it's a pretty easy fix."

His father chuckled. "If you say so, young lady. I'll have to take your word for it, because I hate to admit it but I don't know a thing about engines."

Callie laughed. "That's okay, that's why you have me!" Pride filled her voice and as Landon smiled down on her, his eyes sparkled brightly.

"Lucky us." The words were out of his mouth before he had time to think about them and the moment that Callie and his father turned to look at him, he felt heat rising in his cheeks. Clearing his throat, he shuffled in his spot, while staring down at his feet. "I just meant…"

Laughter shook his father's shoulders. "We know son. Now, you two better get going if you're going to be ready for the Pierce Family Christmas Tree Decorating Extravaganza later today."

Callie's eyes grew wide as she glanced between the two men. "The what?"

Landon's lips curled upwards and he chuckled, drawing her eyes back to him. "I'll tell you about it in the car. But first I need to go grab a few things. Meet back here in ten?"

Callie nodded and then skipped back towards the cabin, leaving Landon and his father staring after her. Silence surrounded them for a moment before his father slapped him across the back. "It's nice to see you enjoying a lady's company again, son." At his father's comment, Landon's eyes widened while he shook his head in denial but his dad continued before Landon could speak. "Never mind me, son. I'm an old man, what do I know?" Sarcasm dripped from his words as he winked and then strolled back towards the cabin, leaving Landon staring after him.

Ten minutes later, Landon was in his SUV with the heat on and Christmas music playing quietly when the passenger door opened and Callie climbed in.

"Hey!" Her lips were spread into a wide grin and her whole face was glowing, which prompted a flutter to dance across Landon's chest. She had taken her hair out of the pony tail and it was cascading freely down onto her shoulders. Two short pieces framed either side of her face and her pink sparkling lips shone under the morning sun, and as the flutter danced across his chest, Landon found himself thinking again, how beautiful she was.

As he sat appreciating her beauty, he smiled back at her. "Hey. I um… you look…sorry. I mean, I was just trying to get us some heat."

Callie giggled, and Landon assumed she was

giggling at his awkwardness causing him to groan inwardly. But as he watched her strap her seatbelt on and then offer him a soft, warm smile, he felt himself relax.

"Thanks. And thanks for driving me into town."

Shifting the car into gear, Landon started backing out of the driveway as he shook his head, glancing at her briefly. "No thanks needed. You're the one doing us a favour. But are you sure you don't mind doing this? It is your vacation."

Callie, whose eyes had been focused in front of her turned to meet his gaze. "I don't mind at all. In fact, I'm excited. It's what I love to do."

Landon held his gaze on her for a moment before returning his eyes to the rear-view mirror. "I've been wondering about that. How did you become a mechanic? I mean, it isn't a job that most women would be interested in doing, let alone be as enthusiastic about it as you."

His comments incited her laughter to fill his car. "I know. I get that a lot. In fact, on the way up here, Jade told me that it was nice to see me out of my coveralls because I actually looked like a woman for a change."

Landon turned wide eyes on her. "She did not?"

Laughing, she nodded. "She did. You know your sister."

A groan escaped his throat. "Oh god."

"It's okay, though. I don't mind. She isn't wrong. If you see me at work with the guys, most of the time you can't tell I am a woman until you get close. I don't mind though. I like being one of the guys."

That last statement piqued his curiosity. "Oh yeah?"

"Yeah. When I was in school and when I first started at the dealership, it was difficult because most people didn't think I could do as good a job as the guys. But now, I've been there for a few years and I have their respect and most of the time, I don't have an issue with customers."

The tone of her voice dimmed during the last part of her sentence, causing his eyebrows to raise. He turned his gaze to her. "Issue? What kind of issues would you have?"

She sighed and then turned forward so that she was watching the world pass them by. "Well, sometimes, when they see me, they request that I not be the one to work on their car."

Turning wide eyes towards her, Landon's voice was enveloped in disbelief. "People actually say that?"

She nodded but kept her focus on the world in front of her. "They do, on occasion. And it took me a long time to learn to not take it personally."

"What do your co-workers say?"

At his question, Callie turned her focus back on him. Her lips were curled upwards but there was a hint of sadness in her eyes. "They always defend me, especially my boss. But..."

"But it still hurts."

Sighing, she nodded. "Yeah. And I wish it didn't but I can't help it."

"Callie, of course, it hurts. Being a woman doesn't mean you can't do the same things that a man can do."

"Exactly." She turned her eyes away for a moment and when she turned them back on him, they were sparkling brightly. "Thanks for that Landon."

He shook his head. "You don't have to thank me. It's the truth." He offered her a warm smile and she smiled shyly back in return. After a moment, he turned his attention back to the road in front of them. "Okay, so, back to my original question. How did you get into this line of work?"

"Pops."

The moment the word was out of her mouth, recollection dawned in his mind. "Right. I remember you saying something about you helping him after school."

"Yeah. Everyday I would go to the garage where he worked and if I didn't have homework, I would help him and he talked to me about what he was working on and explained everything he was doing. He was a patient man and a great teacher." Her voice was soft and Landon could hear love mixed with a hint of nostalgia encasing her words.

He let a moment of silence settle between them before speaking again. "And you fell in love with fixing cars?"

She turned to meet his gaze and he could see joy spreading across her face. "I did. Most people don't get paid to do what they love. I'm lucky."

Staring at her joyous reflection, Landon felt a tug on his heart as she beamed up at him. His lips curled upwards and he nodded as he turned his attention back to the road. "You are lucky and I am too. That's the same way I feel about my job."

"You enjoy pulling over crazy speeders and having to interrupt bar fights?" Her words were cloaked in amusement and when he glanced at her, he witnessed laughter dancing in her eyes.

"Well, when it involves beautiful women, then yes." His eyes were sparkling as they gazed down on her and as they did, he saw a pink hue colour her cheeks. Silence surrounded them then, as they both turned their attention back to the outside world. After several minutes, Callie cleared her throat.

"So, um, how long have you been on the force?"

"Almost twenty years, now. I joined the academy right out of high school."

"Wow!" Amazement blanketed her words, prompting a sense of pride to wash over him, but then a smirk formed quickly across his lips.

"I know, right? I'm old." Laughter framed his words and when he moved his teasing eyes from the road to her, he caught her rolling her eyes, which he noted were swimming with admiration.

"Funny. That's not what I meant, Officer."

Laughter touched his eyes. "I know, I'm sorry. I couldn't resist."

She stared at him trying to look annoyed but then a giggle escaped her throat. "Okay, fair enough. But seriously, twenty years. That's amazing." He nodded as she tilted her head and her eyes filled with curiosity.

"Did you always want to be a cop?"

The moment the question entered his ears, dark memories filled his thoughts and a dark shadow itself cast over him as his grip on the steering wheel tightened. When he responded, his voice was low and devoid of the laughter from a moment ago. "Not always, not until I was sixteen."

As the atmosphere in the SUV suddenly changed, Callie reached across the center console, and placed her hand gently on his arm. He glanced down at her hand and then up into her soft, concerned eyes. "Landon, what happened?"

Realizing that his darkened demeanor had signaled her that there was a dark story in his past, he took a deep breath, exhaling it slowly before making his confession. "I had an accident when I was sixteen and someone was killed."

A gasp escaped her lips, causing his eyes to droop and his shoulders to sag but she quickly shook her head. "Landon, I'm so sorry."

"Don't be. I was the one driving the car. It was dark and rainy and they ruled it an accident but I killed someone, you don't get over that easily. So, when I turned eighteen, I joined the academy. I wanted to help people, to spend my life making up for that life I took."

"Landon…"

He shook his head, quickly stopping her before she could continue. A sheepish smile touched the corners of his mouth but the dark misery still lingered in his eyes. "I'm sorry, Callie. I didn't mean to put a damper on our day."

She shook her head, compassion filling her eyes. "Landon, you didn't. I'm just sorry that happened to you. And I'm here if you want to talk about it."

He shook his head again, desperate to change the subject. "Thank you but it was a long time ago and although it took me a long time, I made my peace with it, so let's just forget about it. Okay? We have cars to repair and Christmas trees to decorate." His voice was slightly strained but he attempted to sound as chipper as possible.

He could feel Callie's eyes lingering on him for a moment before he heard her soft, sweet voice beside him. "Okay, consider it forgotten. Now, are you going to tell me about the Pierce Family Christmas Tree Decorating Extravaganza?"

Landon's lips curled upwards as his eyes focused on her for a moment before he pried them away to focus on the road in front of him. His grip on the steering wheel relaxed as he let his mind focus on Christmas instead of the horrors of the past. "It's one of the Pierce family Christmas traditions."

"Pierce family Christmas traditions?" Curiosity framed her question.

"Yup. Last night was the first night so it was classic Christmas children's movies, tonight is tree decorating, and tomorrow is Christmas charades."

"Wow!"

Landon laughed at her wide eyes. "I know, right? We do an activity every night leading up to Christmas."

"Oh, my goodness! That's amazing!" Joy sang through her voice and Landon grinned, keeping his eyes focused on the road.

"I suppose. I always thought it was a lot, but the kids enjoy it and everyone else does too, I guess."

Tilting her head towards him, her eyebrows raised slightly. "So, do you guys do this every year. Take two weeks off and spend it together at the cabin?"

"Most of us do. I usually work, so I come up on my days off, and everyone else comes up when they can. We try to be here for the week before Christmas, at least. It depends on if and when we can all get away from work."

Callie shook her head as amazement flashed in her eyes. "I think that's really cool."

Landon nodded. "What about you? I know you said that it was always just you and your Pops but did you have any Christmas traditions?" He focused his eyes on hers for a brief moment and when he did, he noticed a hint of nostalgia, mixed with sadness reflecting within them.

Offering him a small smile, she nodded. "Yeah. I mean, it wasn't much but every year, Pops would take me to see Santa. It's funny, because I had forgotten all about it until the other day. I was at the mall and the memory of our trips to Santa's Village came flooding back when I stopped to watch the children visiting Santa." Landon's lips curled upwards as she continued to speak with nostalgia touching every word. "Every year, we would get dressed up and head down to the mall. I remember waiting in line, holding Pop's hand as excitement brewed within me. Then, after I told Santa all my wishes for that year and got my picture taken, we would go to a restaurant and have a special sit-down meal. It was one of the few times that we went to an actual restaurant."

Landon's eyes twinkled at the image of her childhood memory. "That sounds like it was really special, Callie."

Her eyes were misted in memory as her lips curled upwards. "It was." A soft sigh slipped through her lips. "I miss him."

Landon, unsure how to respond, simply nodded and when Callie turned her gaze back to the world outside, silence fell over them. As they drove the rest of the way into town in silence, Landon's thoughts were on that little girl, who had so many loses in her young life, but had grown up to be the amazing young woman sitting beside him now.

Chapter 9

When Landon and Callie reached the auto parts store, they were in and out quickly. Callie knew exactly what she needed and where to find it and after arguing at the counter, Landon eventually conceded and let her pay for the parts. After a couple more stops that included his mother's favourite bakery and Callie's house to grab some tools, Landon pointed his SUV in the direction of the mountain but when he felt hunger pains growling in his stomach, a different idea caught traction in his mind. Turning his attention to the passenger seat, he tilted his head, with a question touching the corners of his eyes. "Hey, since we missed breakfast, do you want to go grab a bite to eat?"

A wide grin immediately materialized across Callie's lips. "That's a great idea. I'm starving. I ate a banana before we left but it wasn't quite enough."

Nodding, Landon offered her a smile of agreement. "Yeah, for me either. But I know this great place on the way out of town. It's a little off the beaten track but worth the few extra minutes."

"Sounds good. I'm in!" Enthusiasm enveloped her words and before long, Landon was pulling his SUV into the parking lot of 'Diner 5'. It was an older, stucco building, with large windows and a big sign on the roof that was in desperate need of a paint job.

He watched her survey her surroundings as they strolled towards the entrance. The Diner was a few miles off the highway and stood alone in what seemed like the middle of no where. As her wide, curious eyes landed on him, she raised an eyebrow. "How do you know about this place?"

He offered her a warm smile. "It's a favourite amongst the guys."

Callie nodded as she surveyed the parking lot until her eyes fell on the three police cars parked at the side of the building. "Oh." She turned her attention back to him and as he stared at her, he felt his heart rate increase as his breath caught in his throat. Her big brown eyes were shimmering under the late morning sunshine and her shiny pink lips drew his attention right to them. Staring down at her lips, he found himself longing to feel them against his own and as that inappropriate thought entered his mind, he felt heat creeping up his neck onto his cheeks. He quickly glanced away from her, clearing his throat as he did.

"Oh, yeah. Looks like a few of the guys are here." Bringing his eyes back to meet hers, he tilted his head slightly. "We can go somewhere else, if you want?"

A look of surprise filled her eyes, which quickly turned to concern. Her eyes dropped down to survey her body before they met his again. "Oh, um, well…if you would rather not go in. I um…" As she fumbled on her words, he heard a hint of hurt enter her voice, causing his stomach to drop.

Reaching out, he placed a reassuring hand on her arm and locked his eyes onto hers. "That's not it, Callie, that's not what I meant. It's just, once the guys see us, we'll end up sitting with them and I wasn't sure if you'd be okay with that."

As his words registered in her mind, he saw the concern vanish from her eyes as she shook her head. "I don't mind. I think it could be interesting to meet some of your colleagues." He watched as the corners of her mouth curled into a smirk and a twinkle began to glint in her eyes. "Maybe they'll have some good stories to tell me about you."

A groan slipped through his lips. "Oh god! Yeah, maybe this is a bad idea."

Callie shook with laughter and then grabbed his hand and led him towards the entrance. The moment his large frame wedged through the door, he heard his name being hollered from a booth in the corner of the busy restaurant.

"Landon, over here buddy."

He nodded towards the table before turning his full attention on Callie. "Ready?"

Her eyes were twinkling up at him as her lips curled into a wide grin. "Yup, are you?" Amusement framed her words and Landon groaned again.

"Not at all. But let's go." Grabbing her hand, he led her towards the guys, dropping her hand just before they reached the table, which was occupied by three of his colleagues; all three of whom had been on the job with him for years and had been by his side at Izzie's funeral.

"Hey guys. How's the day going?"

Josh, one of his closest friends and colleagues grinned from Landon to Callie and then back to Landon. "Pretty good. But not as good as yours apparently." Amusement enveloped his words as he winked at Landon.

At his friend's unspoken insinuation, Landon felt his heart thump against his chest and when he turned his gaze to Callie, he could see a pink hue brightening her cheeks. Turning his eyes back to his colleagues, he cleared his throat, before starting the introductions. "Guys, this is Callie Anderson. She works with Jade. She's spending Christmas with us at the cabin."

They all nodded and then extended their hands out. Callie smiled brightly at the three of them and Landon would have given anything to know what she was thinking in that moment.

"It's nice to meet you all." Her voice was sweet as she surveyed the three men.

Josh grinned down at her, and Landon could see the wheels turning in Josh's head. "You too, Callie." As her name left Josh's lips, Landon saw a twinkle form in his friend's eyes, as a smirk began to slowly spread from the corners of his mouth. "Wait. Callie? You mean Callie Anderson, bar fight girl?"

Landon felt his heart stop as Josh's wide amused eyes landed on him. But before Landon could respond, he heard Callie's voice pipe up beside him.

"Bar fight girl?" Curiosity, enveloped in amusement laced her words and Landon could feel the crimson of his warm cheeks.

Shooting daggers at Josh, before turning his attention to Callie, Landon shook his head. "I don't know what he's talking about."

Callie grinned, eyeing him suspiciously before turning her gaze back to Josh. She raised an eyebrow and Landon could see the question in her eyes so he quickly stepped forward, addressing Josh as he did. "Don't you guys have somewhere to be?"

Mischief glimmered in Josh's eyes as he and their other two colleagues laughed. Josh then stood up holding his hands up in front of him. "Okay, I can take a hint." He bowed his head towards Callie as the other guys stood up beside him. "It was a pleasure to meet you, Callie."

She nodded, offering the three of them a warm smile. "You as well. And be safe out there."

Josh tipped his hat in her direction. "We always are!" Then he, followed by his colleagues shuffled out of the booth.

After watching the guys exit the building, Callie and Landon slid into the booth across from each other. As Landon picked up a menu, he could feel Callie's eyes on him. When he glanced up, she was staring at him with a glint of amusement shining in her eyes and a mischievous smirk curving her lips. "Bar fight girl, hey? You were talking about me?"

Landon groaned. "Josh has a big mouth."

A laugh escaped Callie's lips, but she didn't press the issue further, allowing relief to flood through Landon's body. He went back to staring at his menu as Callie removed her coat, revealing a tight pink sweater underneath, which clung to her chest, and unintentionally drew Landon's eyes downwards. As his eyes lingered a little longer than they should have, his thoughts flashed to the dress that she had been wearing the first night they had met and as he did, he could feel heat rise through his body. When he pulled his eyes back up to her face, he was relieved to see that she was looking around the restaurant and hadn't noticed his inappropriate staring.

"This is a neat little place. Gives me a bit of a fifties vibe."

When Callie's focus returned to him, he swallowed the lump of guilt that had formed in his throat and then nodded while sweeping his eyes across the room. She was right; the entire room was filled with red fabric booths and the jukebox in the corner looked like an antique. "Yeah, and the food is pretty good too. Like grandma's home cooking."

Callie smiled and licked her lips, and as she did, Landon found himself thinking about kissing her again. 'Stop that.' He yelled at himself silently and then shook his head before focusing his eyes back down on the menu in front of him. Luckily Callie didn't seem to notice any of his weird behavior as she stared down at her own menu.

Silence surrounded them after that until the waitress came by to take their orders, after which, Callie turned their conversation towards talk about his father's car. The neutral topic of discussion was welcome, as Landon needed something to distract him from thinking about kissing her.

After breakfast, they headed back up the mountain, and the moment they pulled into the driveway of the cabin, Callie jumped out of the SUV and sprung towards the front door; excitement radiating off of her. As she reached the top step of the porch, she turned back towards him; a bright smile touching her lips and joy shining in her eyes. "I'm just gonna go change and then I'll start on the car."

Landon grinned at the pure joy in her voice. "Do you need a helper?"

"Absolutely!" Her eyes sparkled as she nodded enthusiastically.

"Good. I'll go change too and meet you at dad's

car."

"Sounds good." Her reply was quick and within seconds she had disappeared into the cabin, leaving Landon standing alone, beaming widely at the closed door.

Chapter 10

Ten minutes later, dressed in the grease-stained coveralls that she had picked up from home that morning, Callie was organizing her tools in the garage behind the cabin where they had decided to work, when she heard a small, quizzical voice behind her.

"Callie, *you're* fixing Pop's car?"

Turning around, Callie found Scarlet's small, wide, gray eyes staring up at her. They were filled with both disbelief and curiosity.

Callie's lips curled upwards, as she crouched down to be eye level with Scarlet. "I am. And your dad is going to help me."

Scarlet's eyes moved to her father, who smiled down at her from his position on the other side of the workbench from Callie. She then returned her gaze to Callie. "Can I help too?"

"Um, sure." Callie tried to hide the surprise from her tone as she glanced up at Landon. "As long as it's okay with your dad."

Scarlet squirmed with excitement, and she turned her eyes up towards her father. "Can I daddy? Please? I'll be careful."

Landon's lips curled upwards, and his eyes sparkled under the rays of the afternoon sun that were glimmering in through the open garage door. "Of course. But you have to do exactly what Callie tells you, okay?"

Scarlet nodded. "I promise." Her young voice was

serious when she answered and when Callie glanced back down at her, she grinned at the joy flickering in Scarlet's eyes.

"Okay. Then I guess, Callie you now have two helpers." Callie's eyes flickered up towards Landon when he spoke and they held each other's gaze for a moment until Scarlet drew their attention back to her.

"Yayyy!!" She started jumping up and down and Callie stood up, grinning widely as she turned her gaze back to Landon.

"Well, then, helpers." Her eyes roamed down to Scarlet. "Shall we get this show on the road? We have a Christmas tree to decorate later."

Scarlet grinned happily, revealing her gap-toothed smile and Callie beamed down at her. Then the three of them set about fixing Nick's car. It was a simple job for Callie and as she worked, she made sure to explain everything she was doing to Scarlet, just like her grandfather had done for her. It made the job take longer than normal but Callie didn't mind. And as she spoke, Scarlet was wide eyed, listening carefully to everything Callie told her and passing Callie tools whenever she requested them. As Callie worked on the car and talked to Scarlet, Landon tucked himself into a corner, but Callie could sense his eyes on her as he watched her and his daughter work.

Once the repair was complete, Landon sent Scarlet into the house to shower off the dirt and grease while he assisted Callie with the clean up of the garage and tools.

As she worked, Callie glanced in his direction. "I sure am glad we had this garage to work in."

Landon, glancing up from the other side of the room, where he was stacking some tools, offered her a wide grin. "Me too. It would have been a bit cold to do it out there." He motioned towards the window behind her, and her gaze followed his.

When she turned her eyes back to him, there was a twinkle forming within them. "Yeah. We probably would have frozen our butts off."

A loud laugh slipped through Landon's lips and his eyes were dancing as he nodded in agreement, with a smirk touching the corners of his mouth. "Amongst other things."

Callie tilted her head as confusion flickered in her eyes, but that confusion was quickly replaced with understanding, prompting a giggle to float out of her mouth. "Oh, yeah. I'm thinking that would have been a bit of a problem for one of us." Amusement framed her words and he nodded, grinning widely.

"Yup."

Laughter filled the garage as they both enjoyed the moment, and as they continued working and their laughter died down, Landon strolled to the side of the garage where she was working and leaned against the wall, drawing her eyes towards him. His eyes were full of appreciation, prompting her to tilt her head and smile, eyeing him with curiosity. "What?"

"Thank you." The two words were completely enveloped in appreciation as they entered the air between them.

Callie straightened up and as she leaned against the work bench behind her, she folded her arms across her chest, tilting her head again. "For what?"

"For your patience with Scarlet. You were amazing with her." Admiration surrounded his words and lit his eyes.

Callie dipped her eyes down shyly as she replied softly. "It was nothing."

"No, it was something. You took the time to show her everything you were doing. I think that was amazing."

Appreciation was swimming in her eyes when she lifted them back up to meet his gaze. "Well, I don't know about amazing but it's how I was taught. So, if it was amazing you have my Pops to thank."

Landon's lips curled upwards as his eyes held hers. Neither of them spoke and after a few moments, they went back to their work until the garage was as clean as it had been when they started.

Chapter 11

After a quick shower to wash away the grease from Nick's car, Callie climbed into her comfy yoga pants and over-sized pink sweatshirt and ambled down the stairs, following the laughter that was echoing throughout the cabin. She was beaming at the cheerful sound touching her ears as she entered the living room, and when her eyes took in the joyous scene greeting her, a wave of happiness washed over her. She stood in the doorway surveying the scene and giggled when she realized that everyone in the room was wearing a colourful ugly Christmas sweater. Her eyes danced with laughter at the sight of Landon in his green Santa sweater and she was so caught up in her amusement that she didn't hear Nick sneak up behind her.

"They are a loud bunch, aren't they?"

Whirling around at the sound of his voice, Callie placed her hand over her chest and let out a surprised gasp. "Oh Nick, hey. I didn't hear you there."

Nick offered her an apologetic smile while chuckling softly. "Sorry, dear. I didn't mean to sneak up on ya."

Taking a moment to allow her heart rate to drop back down, Callie smiled and then shook her head. "It's okay. I was just enjoying this." She swept her hand out in front of her to indicate what 'this' she was referring to.

Nick scoffed but Callie could see pride twinkling in his eyes. And when he replied he tried to sound gruff, but Callie could hear a hint of amusement mixed with pride surrounding his tone. "Enjoying? You must be a gluten for punishment. All this noise and carrying on is enough to drive an old guy to drink."

Laughter danced in her eyes while a smile touched her lips. "Well, maybe I am a little bit of a gluten for punishment, but I like it."

Nick glanced around the room at his family and then met her gaze with his, pride still flickering in his eyes. His voice was hushed when he responded. "Don't tell anyone but, so do I."

A surprised laugh escaped her lips as she nodded and then used her finger to make a cross over her heart. "Your secret is safe with me, cross my heart."

Nick chuckled again and then shot a wink in her direction. "Good girl!" They grinned happily at each other after that and then he turned his attention back to the group in front of them. "Now, what are you waiting for? Go in there and join the party."

Giggling, she nodded and then strode into the room, assessing the activity around her. Jade and Elliott were in a corner, untangling Christmas lights, Tasha was sitting on the floor around the coffee table with all the kids, big bowls of popcorn laid out in front of them, and Mike and Landon were trying to get the large tree to stand up straight in it's tiny stand. She watched the two men for a moment while allowing the scent from the logs crackling in the wood-burning fireplace to fill her nostrils. As she continued to venture further into the room, the excited sound of Scarlet's voice touched her ears.

"Callie, Callie. Come sit with me and help us make the popcorn garland." Scarlet scooted over on the floor, making room between her and her cousin as she beamed up at Callie, with excitement dancing in her eyes.

Callie grinned happily down at her little helper, who along with Lara and Britney was wearing reindeer antlers on the top of her head, a sight that filled Callie with Christmas joy. Her lips curled upwards as she knelt down and planted herself beside Scarlet. "I like your antlers, ladies." She glanced between the three girls and they all offered her proud smiles in return, then she returned her focus to Scarlet. "That looks like fun, Scarlet. I've never made popcorn garland before."

Scarlet's eyes widened as she stared up at her. "Never?"

Callie shook her head. "Nope, never." Grabbing a piece of string from the table, Callie focused her eyes on Scarlet. "Will you show me?"

A wide smile spread across Scarlet's lips, touching her sparkling eyes. "Yes!" The excitement in Scarlet's little voice sent a shot of joy through Callie's heart.

As Scarlet began to show Callie how to make the popcorn garland, Callie stole a glance at Tasha, who was watching her niece and Callie with appreciation welling in her eyes. When Callie's eye caught Tasha's, Tasha nodded and mouthed the words thank you. Callie simply nodded back and offered Tasha a warm smile. They held each other's focus for a moment before Callie turned her attention back to Scarlet, who was talking excitedly beside her.

A short while later, after Callie had made one very long strand of popcorn garland all by herself, Courtney and Nick entered the room carrying trays of hot chocolate and the sweet treats that Callie and Landon had picked up from the bakery that morning.

"Okay, everyone. It's time to get this tree decorated." As the words left Courtney's mouth all the children began to buzz excitedly, prompting Callie to smile happily as a burst of joy shot through her.

Standing up, she maneuvered herself to the side of the room, allowing the children to crowd around Courtney to grab their treats. As she was watching the happy faces of the children, she sensed a presence beside her and when she turned to look, she found Landon leaning against the wall beside her with his arms folded across the Santa sweater that clung to his muscular chest. He was beaming at the scene in front of them.

"They're pretty excited, aren't they?" He didn't turn his eyes away from the children when he spoke.

Callie nodded and then turned her attention back to the center of the room. "Yes, they are. But I have to admit, I am too."

"Oh yeah?"

Turning her gaze back to him, she found herself staring into his twinkling, dark gray eyes and was lost in them for a moment before she quickly found her voice. "Yeah. Well, Pops wasn't much for decorating."

Landon straightened slightly and she noticed a crease of concern form across his forehead. "You mean, you didn't decorate for Christmas growing up, like no tree?"

She replied quickly with a shake of her head. "No, we had a tree." She paused and turned her eyes towards his family around them. "It just wasn't like this."

"Chaos, you mean?" The joke came off his lips enveloped in warmth, prompting Callie to smile as she turned her gaze back to meet his.

"Exactly. Usually, it was just me decorating. Pops would be off working in the garage or something." She tried not to sound sad, but she knew that there was a hint of sadness in her eyes because Landon's lips curled downwards, and his eyes drooped slightly.

"I'm sorry, Callie."

She quickly shook her head again as a rush of embarrassment washed over her. "No, it's okay. I'm sorry. I don't mean to be a downer. I'm just really excited to be here, doing this with all of you." She held his gaze for a moment as the corners of her mouth slowly curved into a smirk. "And, I'm loving that sweater you have on, Officer Pierce."

A groan slipped through Landon's lips, but his eyes were twinkling as he stared down at her. Then, a smirk slowly began to spread across his lips and he grabbed her hand and led her towards the rest of the group, which was now crowded around the tree. As they approached, Courtney greeted them holding a wrapped gift box in her hands.

"For you, Callie." Courtney's eyes sparkled as she handed the gift to Callie.

Callie's eyes widened and a gasp of shock escaped her lips. "Really?" As Courtney nodded, Callie offered her a warm smile and then slowly opened the box. The moment the presents' contents revealed themselves, a loud laugh flew out of Callie's mouth. Glancing up at the rest of the group, she pulled her present out for them all to see.

"It's your very own Pierce ugly Christmas sweater." Pride and love enveloped Courtney's words as Callie held the sweater up against her chest and rested her eyes on Courtney. A tear pooled in Callie's eyes as a feeling of joy and love washed over her. "I love it. Thank you!"

Courtney smiled and then turned to the rest of her family, gesturing towards the tree. "Well, gang, shall we do this?"

Cheers sounded throughout the room as everyone began pulling decorations out of boxes. Callie watched them for a moment and then pulled her new sweater over her head. As she did, she felt Landon's eyes on her.

"Nice sweater, Miss Anderson!" His voice held a tone of teasing prompting her to grin up at him.

"Thank you, Officer. I think this may be my favourite sweater ever."

Landon's eyes sparkled as he stared down at her and grinned. "I think it looks great on you."

Her lips curled upwards and they held each other's gaze for a few moments before joining the others at the tree. The sadness that had flickered in Callie's eyes and in her heart earlier was gone, replaced by a feeling of warmth and love as she laughed, joked and enjoyed the Pierce family Christmas tree decorating tradition.

After the last decoration was added, everyone stood back as Nick pointed the remote that controlled the lights at the tree. "Okay, is everyone ready?" A chorus of yes' rang out around the room, prompting Nick to look around and smile widely. "Okay, on the count of five. One, two..."

"Three, four, five." Everyone counted as excitement buzzed around them. Callie glanced around as she counted, wanting to implant this special memory into her mind. When she turned her attention back to the tree, the glow of twinkling, colourful lights filled her eyes, revealing their beautifully decorated masterpiece.

Later that night, after everyone had gone upstairs to bed, Callie wandered back down to the living room. Making herself comfortable on the end of the couch, she stared at the twinkling lights and homemade decorations and basked in the warmth and love that enveloped the Pierce family Christmas cabin.

Chapter 12

Lounging under the warm, down comforter of the most comfortable bed she had ever laid in, Callie stared out the window as the morning light peeked in. When she had finally pulled herself away from the Christmas tree the night before, she had decided to leave the curtains open, which was now giving her an unobstructed view of the beautiful world outside. As she watched tiny, white, ice crystals cascading down from the sky, from her cozy bed, her thoughts wandered to the night before and she could still feel the joy of being included in the family activities. Reaching her arms above her head, she stretched her body and was thinking about rolling over and going back to sleep when she heard something connect with the windowpane. Focusing her eyes, she could see the remnants of a snowball as it melted down the glass. As she watched the streak of snow slide down, another snowball came flying through the air, striking the glass with a thud.

"What the heck?" As confusion creased her forehead, Callie climbed out of bed and ambled over to the window to see what was happening outside. The moment her eyes focused on the yard beneath her, a wide smile touched the corners of her lips. Opening the window, she stuck her head outside. "Well, good morning, Officer Pierce and Miss Scarlet. What are you two trouble makers up to?"

Landon, who was dressed in a black parka and jeans with a black toque perched on his head and black gloves warming his hands, placed a hand over his heart and stuck his lower lip out as he stared up at her. "Trouble maker? Why Miss Anderson, you wound me."

A surprised snort flew from Callie's mouth causing

heat to rise in her cheeks and prompting both Landon and Scarlet to shake with laughter.

"That was very lady like." Landon teased her with a smirk curving the corners of his mouth.

Callie shook her head while rolling her eyes. "Funny. But seriously, what's going on?"

Callie's question was directed at Landon, but it was Scarlet's voice that rang out from below. "We're gonna build a snow fort and we wanted to see if you want to help us."

Callie's lips curled upwards as she turned her eyes to Scarlet. "I've never built a snow fort before. That sounds like fun."

Scarlet's pink toque covered head bobbed up and down enthusiastically. "It is. Come help us." The words rolled out of Scarlet's mouth as a demand, not a request, prompting both Callie and Landon to chuckle softly.

Giving Scarlet a salute, Callie smiled down at her. "Yes, ma'am. I'll be down in five minutes."

Scarlet beamed happily up at her and then Callie closed the window and quickly went about getting ready.

Five minutes later, she stumbled out of the house with her matching pink boots, jacket, and mittens firmly in place. As she descended the stairs and glanced around the front yard, she didn't see her two friends anywhere. She stood staring at the world around her with confusion touching her eyes, as snowflakes floated onto her coat and hair. When she heard the high-pitched squeal of Scarlet's giggles, the confusion turned to joy. Following the sound of Scarlet's excitement, she found her friends in the large, snow-covered yard behind the cabin. They were both on their knees, piling up snow, wearing wide, happy grins. She quickly trudged through the snow towards them, wearing her own wide, happy grin.

"Hey you two. Can I join the fun?"

At the sound of her voice, Scarlet's little head whipped up, revealing bright pink cheeks and a wide joyous smile. "Hi Callie!"

"Hey Scarlet. Wow, your cheeks are as pink as your jacket."

Scarlet's eyes twinkled and her smile widened as she pointed at Callie. "And your jacket too."

Looking down at herself, Callie grinned and then turned her eyes back to her young friend. "Oh, yeah. You're right. We're like twins."

Callie's response prompted a squeal to escape Scarlet's lips and she clapped her hands in excitement. "Yayyy!" Turning her attention towards her father, who was busy piling snow, she bounced up and down on her knees, excitement radiating out of her. "Daddy, did you hear that? Callie and I are twins!"

The excitement in Scarlet's voice elicited smiles from both Callie and Landon as Landon nodded. "I see that. So, what do you say, twins? Should we get this snow fort built?"

Scarlet nodded enthusiastically and got back to work as Callie knelt down beside her. "Okay, well, I've never built a snow fort before Scarlet, so you'll have to show me what to do."

Scarlet's lips curled upwards, and she nodded and then proceeded to show Callie how to pack the snow onto the structure that her and her father had already begun building. Callie watched and before long, she was making quick work of her section of the fort as snowflakes continued to fall gently down around them.

After an hour, of laughing and working, Landon managed to convince Scarlet, whose lips were starting to turn purple from the frosty air, that it was time to go inside. She whined and argued until she found out that her cousins were making gingerbread men with their grandmother. That information enticed her to skip happily towards the house with Callie and Landon following close behind.

As they marched through the snow, Callie felt Landon's eyes on her. Turning to meet his gaze, she smiled up at him. He returned her smile as his eyes softened with appreciation. "Thank you for that."

A wrinkle of confusion touched her forehead. "For what?"

His eyes twinkled and he glanced around at the world around them, before turning his gaze back to her. "For building the snow fort with us. I think my daughter really enjoyed it."

Curling her lips, Callie nodded. "You're welcome. But I'm the one that should be saying thank you. I had a lot of fun. I've never done that before. So, thank you."

The corners of Landon's mouth flipped upwards and the twinkle in his eye sparkled brightly. "Well, you're welcome. I had fun too!"

They held each other's gaze for a moment, and then

silence followed them as they continued their walk back to the house. Just as they were rounding the corner from the back yard, a small snowball came flying towards them, hitting Landon's right leg.

"What the?" Surprise encapsulated Landon's words as he set wide eyes on Callie. Callie, whose eyes were equally wide, focused her gaze on the direction that the snowball had come from, just in time to see another snowball heading straight for her. She tried to dodge it, but it connected with her shoulder before she could make a clean getaway. As she was recovering from the snowball attack, her eyes focused on Scarlet, whose little pink face was grinning widely up at both Callie and her father.

"Oh, I see how it is." Landon's voice penetrated Callie's ears and when she turned her eyes to him, he was bent down, gathering a snow ball of his own. Callie turned her gaze back to Scarlet, who was also bent down making a snowball. Grinning brightly, she watched as the two of them stood up and hurled their snowballs at each other. Scarlet squealed as the snowball hit her stomach and then she ran behind a tree, giggling as she went. When Callie turned her attention back to Landon, he was already making another snowball but this time when he stood up, he flung the snowball at Callie instead of his daughter.

"Hey!" A surprised giggle followed Callie's statement and then she quickly bent down to make her own snowball but before she could send it sailing at him, another snowball pelted her jean covered leg. "Oh, now it's on Officer Pierce." Putting her head down, she quickly packed snow between her hands and as she did, she heard Scarlet's little voice call out.

"I'll help you, Callie."

Glancing up, Callie watched Scarlet running towards her, hurtling snowballs in her father's direction.

Landon laughed and ran behind a tree, before bending down to start making snow balls. As he did, Callie and Scarlet started building up a pile of their own and before long, the three of them were embroiled in a snowball fight. They laughed as the snowballs flew through the air and when both Callie and Scarlet were soaked from the onslaught of snow being hurled in their direction, they called a truce. As they made their way into the warmth of the cabin, all three of them were huffing and puffing but beaming with joy.

Chapter 13

After a nice long, hot shower, to remove the chill from her frozen bones, Callie snuggled up beside the crackling fireplace with a book in hand and a warm, cozy blanket wrapped around her legs. As she stared at the pages in front of her, she could hear chatter and laughter from various rooms in the cabin, but the noise didn't distract her. In fact, she found herself enjoying the sounds as she read the latest adventures of her favourite crime fighting duo while the delicious aroma of dinner filled the cabin air around her.

Dinner, that night, like the other nights, was chaotic, loud, delicious and filled Callie with joy. After dinner was eaten and the dishes cleaned, Tasha corralled everyone into the living room for a slide show that she had prepared of various family activities over the past year. There were groans from the men, but even as they groaned, Callie could see a hint of joy touching their eyes. That is, until a photo from Scarlet's class trip to the zoo flashed across the screen. Tasha had escorted her on the trip because Landon had to work that day and the photo on the screen featured the children and their guardians. As the photo reflected in front of them, Callie glanced at Landon, expecting to see a smile touching his lips, but was surprised to see a dark shadow permeating his eyes and a scowl materializing across his lips, instead. She glanced at the rest of the group and noted that they were all still staring happily at the screen, unaware of the shift in Landon's demeanor. As the photo flipped over to the next one, Landon glanced at his sister, and then his daughter, drawing Callie's gaze with him. After a moment of watching the two of them, Landon strolled quietly, out of the room. Callie, who was the only one that noticed him leave, glanced around her, before silently slipping out as well. Following Landon outside, she found him slumped on the porch swing, with his arms folded over his chest and a scowl across his brow. He didn't look up when she approached, so she wasn't sure if he had heard her come outside, so with a soft and quiet voice, she made her presence known. "Hey. Are you okay?"

"Yeah. I'm fine." Landon's response flew from his lips quickly and as it did, he kept his gaze turned away from her. His voice was gruff and in Callie's opinion he didn't sound the least bit fine.

"Are you sure?"

When he moved his head to stare up at her, Callie could see a mixture of annoyance and darkness lining his eyes. "Why wouldn't I be sure?"

"I don't know. It's just..." The darkness evident in his eyes caused her to stop mid-sentence as she began to think that she was making a mistake confronting him. Shaking her head, she waved her hand in an effort to wipe away her last question. "Never mind, it's nothing. I'm sorry."

Landon stood up and stepped towards her; his gray eyes darkening as he stared at her and shook his head. "It's not nothing, Callie. Just spit it out." A gruff ring of annoyance surrounded his words as he towered over her, causing her to cringe slightly and as she did, Landon backed away; apology immediately penetrating his eyes. "I'm sorry, Callie. I didn't mean..." The gruffness that had enveloped his words a moment ago was gone.

She quickly shook her head. "No, Landon, it's okay. It was my fault, I shouldn't have brought it up, it's just that when you saw that picture of Scarlet's class trip, I thought I saw something in your eyes, like a flash of anger." As heat rose within her, she turned around so that he couldn't see the red creeping onto her cheeks.

And as she stood there, with her back to him, she heard a sad sigh pass through his lips. "You weren't wrong. That is what you saw."

Spinning around quickly, she stared at him with wide, questioning eyes. "Really? Why?"

Letting out a long deep breath, his eyelids dropped and when they fluttered back upwards a moment later, Callie noticed a shadow of sadness masking his eyes. Silence surrounded them as she watched him with anticipation. After several seconds, he took another deep breath, exhaled it slowly and then locked his eyes onto hers.

"I recognized someone, one of the parents." His voice was low and even, like he was struggling to control his emotions.

"Okay?"

"And as soon as I recognized him, the floodgates to unwanted memories flew wide open." Callie nodded as he stopped talking. She watched him turn around and retake his seat on the swing and when he scooted over, leaving room for her beside him, she plopped down onto the swing as well. The swing began to sway as they both stared out at the snow-blanketed yard in front of them. Callie smiled at the snowmen that Scarlet and her cousins had made earlier and as she was staring at the children's creations, Landon's voice rang through her ears. "I've never told anyone this and I didn't think I ever would."

Callie turned so that her full attention was focused on him and as she did, he turned his eyes to her. She regarded him with tenderness and responded with gentleness enveloping her words. "You don't have to tell me about it if you don't want to, but I'm here if you do and I'm a great listener."

A slight smile touched the corners of his mouth. "I don't know what it is about you Callie, but I feel like I can tell you anything and you won't judge me or anyone else."

"It's because I won't."

Landon nodded and the smile remained on his lips. He looked away for a moment and when he returned his gaze to her, the smile was gone and his features had darkened. "Izzie was having an affair."

A loud gasp escaped Callie's mouth before she could stop it and as soon as it did, she quickly covered her mouth with her hands. "I'm sorry." Regret oozed through her words. "I didn't mean to…I just…I mean, I wasn't expecting that."

Landon nodded and then returned his gaze to the yard in front of them. "Neither was I." Misery encompassed those three powerful words.

Callie nodded, knowing that he wasn't talking about her gasp. "I'm sorry, Landon." Gentleness touched her words as they left her lips.

Landon nodded again as he returned his gaze to her. "Thanks. Me too."

Tilting her head, she raised an eyebrow in his direction. "How did you, I mean, when did you…how long did you know?"

"I found out the morning we got her diagnosis."

Callie's stomach dropped at the ache evident in his voice. "Landon...I, I don't know what to say."

He nodded again before he turned his gaze away from her.

"I'm guessing it was the man in the photo?"

She watched his head nod in answer but he didn't speak as silence enveloped them. Callie wasn't sure what to say so she just waited for him to speak again. It was several moments before the sound of his voice broke through the silence between them.

"His name is Parker. He's the father of one of Scarlet's classmates. Both Parker and Izzie were stay at home parents at the time. I don't know much more about him, other than that he's still married, which makes me assume that his wife never found out about the affair."

"How did you find out?"

"By accident. Izzie was in the shower, getting ready for her doctor's appointment, she thought that I had left for work, but I'd forgotten my watch on the dresser, so I came back in to grab it. Her phone was sitting beside my watch and I didn't mean to look, but the screen was lighting up with messages and my eyes were automatically drawn to it." He paused and shook his head. "I wish I hadn't seen it."

There was so much sadness in those last six words that without thinking Callie grabbed his hand to comfort him. Landon turned his eyes to her and offered her a grateful smile as she addressed him softly. "Landon, you don't have to..."

He shook his head. "I want to. I need to. I've never told anyone, not even Izzie."

Callie's eyes widened at his confession. "What?" Surprise enveloped her single word question.

"Well, I mean, I had planned to. After I read the messages and there were a lot of them, I was heartbroken, stunned, angry, all of it. I mean, Izzie was the love of my life. And there she was sending declarations of love to another man." Callie felt her heart crack as he continued with despair evident in his voice. "I went to work and could barely function, but I had a job to do, so I did it and all day I was planning out what I would say to her. But when I got home, she was waiting for me in the living room, tears streaming down her cheeks. And when she told me about the cancer, I knew I couldn't tell her that I knew about Parker, so I buried it. Then six months later I buried her and her secret forever." A tear slid down his cheek which he quickly wiped away. Then he turned his eyes back to the dark night in front of them.

Callie could feel tears brimming in her own eyes. "Landon, I don't know what to say. I'm so sorry."

A tiny scoff escaped his throat and when he spoke, she detected a hint of bitterness surrounding his words. "It isn't your fault."

Her eyes softened and she squeezed his hand. "I know but I'm still sorry. I'm sorry that you had to live with this secret for the past four years, and that you had no one to talk to. And I'm sorry that Izzie did that to you. You didn't deserve that."

As those last words left her lips, Landon turned his gaze back to her and the look of anguish within them threatened to break Callie's heart. "How do you know that? Maybe I did? Maybe I was a terrible husband who didn't give her what she needed, and therefore she had to go find it with another man? I mean, it had to be partly my fault, right? Izzie was a good person, Callie. She wouldn't have done that if I hadn't driven her to it." Sorrow hitched itself to his words as he pleaded with Callie for an answer.

Callie ached for him as anger began to rise up within her. She took a deep breath to suppress that anger and after exhaling slowly she squeezed his hand again. Shaking her head, she locked her eyes onto his. "Landon, no one deserves to be treated like that. If you weren't making Izzie happy, she could have handled the situation a dozen different ways. Having an affair is on her, not you. And I think you know that."

He turned away, nodding slowly. "Yeah, I do, or I thought I did. But then we spent those six months fighting the cancer and then she died and I never got the chance to ask her why. To ask her why she didn't love me anymore?" He turned his tear-filled eyes back on her and Callie felt all of his heart ache as a knot formed in her stomach.

"Landon…" Tears enveloped his name as it left her lips. They held each other's gaze for a moment and then Landon stood up abruptly, wiping the tears from his eyes.

"I'm sorry Callie. I shouldn't have shared all of that with you. I…"

Callie jumped up and grabbed both his hands, grasping them firmly with her own. She stared at him with stern eyes. "Don't do that. I'm glad you shared it with me. You needed to get it out and I know you wouldn't share any of that with your family. You are too good a man to ruin Izzie's memory like that. And you don't have to worry, I won't tell anyone. I promise."

Relief flashed in his eyes and then he offered her another grateful smile. "Thank you, Callie. Thank you for listening. You're right. I think I needed to get that off my chest."

Callie's lips curled upwards into a soft smile as she gazed at him with soft, caring eyes. "You're welcome. Like I said, I'm a great listener. Anytime you need to talk."

The corners of Landon's mouth lifted upwards then, as he stared at her with smiling eyes. "You know, I wasn't sure about you, but you're kind of growing on me." Callie's mouth dropped open and she shook her head as Landon's eyes twinkled with mischief. She shook her head again, while punching his arm lightly. "Oh, I see, you're graduating from speeding to assaulting a police officer. I may end up arresting you, yet."

Callie let out a surprised laugh before punching him again, this punch a little harder than the first one. "Well, Officer Pierce, as far as I know you are off the clock and on top of that you have no witnesses."

Soft laughter shook his shoulders. "Well, Miss Anderson, you are right on both counts so I guess I'll let it go this once."

Callie laughed and shook her head. After a moment, she straightened her lips and glanced up at him, the laughter gone from her eyes. "But on a serious note, Landon. Thank you for sharing that. I'm sure it wasn't easy."

Landon's eyes grew somber and he nodded while speaking in a low, quiet voice, all evidence of laughter gone. "No, it wasn't. And to be honest, I hadn't really thought about it for a long time. I had put it out of my mind when she was going through treatments and I always thought that one day, when she was better, we would talk about it, and I know once she got sick, the affair stopped because she was too weak to do anything but survive. And I let myself think that maybe the cancer was actually a blessing, because it was going to save our marriage. What a fool I was, huh?"

Callie's lips drooped and sorrow filled her eyes as they locked onto his. Her voice was tender when she responded. "I don't think you're a fool at all. I think you were a man, who loved his wife so much that he couldn't imagine living without her. I think that's amazing. An amazing kind of love and if it got you through those six months than I think it was the best way to be."

Landon's lips curled upwards but sadness continued to shine in his eyes. "Thank you, Callie. You know, I did tell her that I knew, in a way."

Callie tilted her head while raising an eyebrow. "Oh yeah?"

"Yeah. I wrote her a letter and read it at her grave."

"Did it help?"

He nodded slowly. "I think so. I mean, after I did it, I was able to let the memory of that fade and all the good times we had, took center stage in my mind." Turning away from her, he took a step towards the edge of the porch, shaking his head sadly. "But now that I think more about it, maybe it didn't help."

"What do you mean?"

121

He shrugged his shoulders as he turned to face her again. "I don't know. I guess, I was just thinking that maybe by allowing myself to forget her infidelity, I immortalized her as a saint. As the only perfect person for me and…" He shrugged his shoulders again. "And maybe that's been keeping me from moving on."

Callie took a breath while digesting his comments. After a moment she slowly shook her head. "I don't know if immortalizing her as a saint was a bad thing." Landon lifted an eyebrow prompting Callie to continue. "I just mean…she was the love of your life, the mother of your incredible daughter. And people make mistakes. As far as you know, she would have regretted the affair and moved passed it, just like you hoped."

Landon shook his head as a tear slipped down his cheek. His voice was hoarse when he responded. "Maybe."

"And I think that people move on when they're ready. Maybe you haven't moved on because you haven't found the right direction, the right person to move on with."

Landon nodded, keeping his gaze on her as a sad smile spread slowly across his lips. "You know Ms. Anderson…you are a very wise woman."

She returned his smile and felt heat touching her cheeks. "Thank you. Just remember this good advice the next time you catch me speeding."

Her response initiated a surprised chuckle to escape his throat. "Or maybe you just shouldn't speed."

His quick retort prompted a giggle to fly through her lips. "Touché." They both laughed again and their eyes locked, just as a loud bang from behind them made them both jump.

"Daddy, Grandma says it's time for charades."
Scarlet's voice sang through the air and they both
turned towards the door, where Scarlet was smiling
brightly up at them.

Landon groaned quietly but offered his daughter a
wide smile. "Okay, sweet pea. We'll be right there."

As soon as Scarlet turned around and the door
slammed behind her, Callie turned her attention back to
Landon. "I take it, charades is not your thing."

Landon groaned again and then made a gesture
towards his large, muscular frame. "Does this body look
like it does charades?"

Callie couldn't keep a laugh from escaping her lips
at the truth of his words. "Well, I'm a master at
charades so you can be my partner."

Landon's eyes sparkled brightly under the light of
the moon as he smiled down at her. And as Callie
stared into his gorgeous, gray eyes, she felt a flutter
dance across her heart.

"Okay, but consider yourself warned. I suck at
charades." And then without waiting for a response,
Landon placed his hand on the small of her back and
guided her back into the cabin.

Chapter 14

By the time Landon led Callie back into the living room, the partners for charades had been decided and not surprisingly, him and Callie had been paired together. Landon glanced at his mother and Jade, who were both wearing mischievous grins and when he shook his head and rolled his eyes, their grins widened substantially.

After Landon and Callie got settled in the room, his mother stood up, catching everyone's attention. "Okay, so the first pair to try their luck at Christmas charades, will be, Landon and Callie." Amusement laced his mother's voice as she smirked and winked in Landon's direction before retaking her seat beside his father.

Shaking his head, Landon grabbed Callie's hand and lifted her up from the couch where she was squeezed in beside Tasha, whispering into her ear as he did. "Do you want to act or guess? And just remember you've been warned."

Callie giggled and then shook her head. "Doesn't matter to me, I'm good with either. What do you prefer?"

Landon released a quiet groan that was meant for her ears only. "A cold beer at the local pub."

Another giggled before she responded, quietly. "Tomorrow. Tonight, we have a game of charades to win."

He rolled his eyes but his lips curled slightly as the thought of going out for a beer with her, whirled around in his mind. As he was preoccupied with that thought, Callie grabbed a clue from the container on the coffee table, and took center stage in the middle of the living room. Unfolding the clue delicately, her lips curled upwards and a glint of joy sparkled in her eyes as she the piece of paper in her hand. After giving him a wink, she used her hands to make the motion of a movie projector.

"It's a movie." He called out and she nodded and then held up three fingers. "Three words." He responded and she nodded again. When she tapped three fingers against her arm, he called out once more. "Third word." Her head bobbed up and down and she grinned widely before stretching her arms above her head, and then slowly lowering them while moving her fingers.

"Twinkling." He called out and she shook her head.

"Sunshine." She shook her head again.

"Snow." His third guess elicited a nod as she pointed her index finger at him.

"Me? You? Person?" She shook her head at all three of his guesses.

"Man?"

Her head bobbed up and down in enthusiastic confirmation.

"Frosty the snowman?"

"Yes!!!" Her lips curled into a smile that touched her eyes as her loud confirmation evoked cheers from his family around them. She then, leapt towards him, flinging her arms around his neck, clearly caught up in the excitement around them. As she embraced him in victory, she whispered close to his ear. "I thought you said you were bad at this."

His eyes shone as he grinned down at her. "I think that was all my partner's doing."

Callie's eyes danced and he watched as a pink hue crept onto her cheeks and as it did, she turned around and made herself comfortable on the couch as Scarlet and his father started their turn. Landon settled himself beside Callie, feeling her warmth around him as they watched Scarlet and his father. And as everyone else took their turns, Landon's thoughts strayed to the conversation that he and Callie had just had and the ease that he felt around her.

After a couple hours of charades, treats and laughter, everyone quickly scattered to different areas of the cabin, leaving only Landon, Callie and Scarlet sitting in the living room.

Scarlet was spread out on the floor playing with a Barbie and as Landon's loving eyes landed on her, she glanced up at him with a question in her eyes. "Daddy, can we watch a movie?"

His lips curled upwards immediately. "Of course."

She grinned happily and then turned her eyes on Callie, who had just picked up a book from the coffee table. "Callie, do you want to watch with us?"

A look of surprise touched Callie's features as she glanced from Scarlet to Landon, but her surprise was quick to vanish and be replaced with a sparkle of joy as she beamed down at Scarlet. "Sure. I'd like that."

"Yayyy!" Scarlet jumped up and down, prompting both Landon and Callie to smile and then the three of them settled onto the couch, with Scarlet wedged in the middle. She skimmed through the movie channels before finding a Christmas princess movie. Landon groaned inwardly at her selection but when Scarlet glanced up at him, he smiled, prompting her to push 'play' on the remote. Then, for the next ninety minutes, the three of them sat in silence watching the characters on the large television screen.

As the credits rolled indicating the end of the movie, Landon and Callie turned their eyes down towards Scarlet, who was curled up beside Landon; her head snuggled against his chest and her eyes shut tight. Landon's lips curled upwards as he glanced at Callie before looking back down at his daughter. They both watched her as she slept until he moved slightly in an effort to wake her up. As he moved, Scarlet sat up and glanced with tired, drooping eyes, from him to Callie.

"Okay, kiddo, I think it's time for bed."

Scarlet stuck her lower lip out. "But daddy, I'm not tired."

He shook his head and opened his mouth to protest but before he could, a yawn stretched across Scarlet's lips. Glancing from his daughter to Callie, whose twinkling eyes met his while they exchanged a smile, he quickly returned his attention to his daughter, replying with an amused chuckle. "Not tired, hey? Yeah, I can see that."

Scarlet rubbed her eyes as another yawn touched her lips. "Only a little."

Her sweet response prompted a giggle from Callie and a wide grin to spread across Landon's lips. Without further discussion he scooped Scarlet up into his arms and carried her towards the stairs as she snuggled her head into his chest. When he began mounting the stairs she lifted her head, peering over his shoulder.

"Daddy, wait."

He stopped immediately at the concern filling Scarlet's voice. "What's wrong sweet pea?"

"I want Callie to tuck me in."

Callie gasped as Landon turned towards her. She stood up from the couch, with shock framing her eyes. Landon gazed at her with a similar look of shock haunting his own eyes. His gaze then moved quickly back down to his daughter. "Really?"

Scarlet nodded, keeping her dark brown eyes focused on Callie. Her voice was soft and sweet when she addressed Callie. "Callie, will you tuck me in?"

Callie was silent for a moment, her wide eyes focused on Scarlet before moving to meet Landon's gaze. As she set her eyes on him, he knew she could see a glimmer of the tear that had formed in the corner of his eyes. As Callie stood in shocked silence, Landon offered her a small, almost imperceptible nod as the corners of his mouth curved upwards. Callie nodded back offering him her own, small smile before turning her gaze back to Scarlet. "Of course, sweetheart. I'd love to."

A wide grin immediately lit up Scarlet's features. "Yayyy!! Will you read me a story too?"

Callie nodded enthusiastically. "Of course."

An excited squeal escaped Scarlet's throat, prompting laughter to shake both Landon and Callie's shoulders. Landon then, turned and began heading back up the stairs with Callie right behind him.

Once Scarlet was settled into bed, she glanced up at him as he stood beside Callie at the side of the bed. "Okay, daddy. You can go."

His eyes widened. "What? But, I…"

"Please daddy. It's girl time now."

A giggle sounded from beside him as he stared down at his daughter in surprise. He watched as Scarlet winked at Callie, prompting Callie's giggle to turn into a full-blown laugh. Callie's eyes met his and they were dancing with laughter as she held her hands palm up, in front of her. She shrugged, offering him an apologetic smile that held the tiniest hint of a smirk. "Sorry, Officer Pierce, but it appears you have no authority here."

Landon's mouth flew open but no words came out. He just looked from Callie to Scarlet and then back to Callie before shrugging his shoulders in defeat. "Okay, fine. I know when I'm not wanted."

Scarlet beamed up at him, her small oval eyes filled with happiness. "Thank you, daddy."

Landon shook his head before turning on his heel and strolling out of the room. He closed the door behind him, leaving it open a crack. And then, instead of heading downstairs, he stood quietly beside the door, listening to the conversation between his daughter and Callie.

"Okay, little lady, now that it's just us girls, what story would you like me to read?" Callie's voice was joyous, prompting a smile to touch Landon's lips. As curiosity enveloped him, he peered through the tiny crack in the open doorway.

Pulling a book out from beneath her covers, Scarlet handed it to Callie. Callie grabbed it in her fingers and gazed down at the old, green hard cover book. As she read the title, a gasp escaped her lips. "Anne of Green Gables?" Her eyes flew up towards Scarlet, who was smiling happily up at her.

"Daddy told me that it was my mommy's favourite when she was little."

Callie's eyes softened as she glanced back down at the book. She stroked the cover gently as if she was connecting with an old friend. Looking back up at Scarlet, her eyes glimmered with tears as she responded quietly. "It was my mom's favourite too."

Scarlet's smile widened, touching her eyes. "It's mine too."

Callie's lips curled at Scarlet's words and then she nodded. "And mine." At Callie's response, Scarlet reached her little hand out and placed it gently on top of Callie's. Callie glanced down at their touching hands and as he watched, Landon felt warmth wash over him. Callie's eyes lingered on their touching hands for a few moments before she glanced back up at Scarlet, who was still beaming happily up at her. After offering Scarlet a warm smile, Callie opened the book to the first page and began reading. She only made it half way through the first chapter before Scarlet's eyelids dropped over her eyes. Closing the book quietly, Callie stood up, placed a gentle kiss on Scarlet's forehead, turned the lamp off and began to tip toe out of the room, sending Landon flying down the stairs, not wanting to be caught eavesdropping.

He was standing, staring out the large, picture window trying to catch his breath when Callie entered

131

the living room. As she strolled silently towards him, he turned his gaze on her; she was sporting a wide, happy smile, which shone brightly in her eyes. His lips curved as he stared down at her with sparkling, appreciative eyes.

"Thank you for that."

She shook her head. "No thanks needed it was my pleasure."

Landon nodded and turned his attention back to the dark night outside. "I don't mean reading. I meant what you said about your mother."

Callie's eyes widened and her mouth flew open. "You heard that?"

Landon nodded, turning back to her, as a flicker of embarrassment touched his eyes. "I was eavesdropping."

Shaking her head, Callie let her gaze fall to the darkness outside. "Don't let Scarlet hear that." A hint of amusement lined her words as her gaze fell back on him.

"I know, right?" Laughter danced in his eyes and she laughed lightly. They stood staring at each other for a moment and then Landon cleared his throat, and motioned towards the couch. Callie followed his movement with her eyes and then climbed onto one end of the couch as Landon sank into the other. Folding her legs underneath her, she maneuvered herself so that she was completely facing him.

"It was true, what I told her."

Landon's lips curled into a soft smile. "I know."

A smirk formed at the corners of her mouth and she tilted her head, raising an eyebrow in his direction. "How?"

"I could tell." His eyes were gentle and so was his voice when he spoke. "There was something in your voice and I could tell you were shocked at first and then…" He shook his head. "I don't know, I could hear the vulnerability surrounding your words."

Placing her elbow on the top of the couch, Callie rested her head on her hand, keeping her eyes locked on his. "I was shocked but then, I felt…" She looked away from him briefly and when she returned her gaze to his, there was a hint of solace touching her eyes. "I felt, like for once in my life, someone understood me. And I know that's weird since Scarlet is only ten but…"

"But she knows what it's like to grow up without a mother."

Callie nodded and then silence settled over the two of them as they held each other's gaze. Landon's gray eyes were gentle as they stared into hers. "Callie, how did your mother, I mean what happened to her? If you don't mind me asking?"

She shook her head as a flicker of sadness appeared in her eyes. "I don't mind. It was a car accident. My mom was an addict and one day…" Her voice trailed off and Landon felt sympathy swallow his heart.

"Callie, I'm sorry."

She shook her head and offered him a soft smile. "Don't be. It was a long time ago."

He nodded as silence enveloped them again. Their eyes remained locked and as he stared into her beautiful brown eyes, he felt a flutter dance across his chest. Without thinking, he reached across the space between them and gently grazed her cheek with his fingers. She closed her eyes and leaned her cheek into his touch and the moment she did, he quickly pulled his hand away. Her eyes snapped open, and when she stared at him with a question in her eyes, he felt heat rise against his cheeks.

Standing up abruptly, he shook his head. "Callie, I'm sorry, I didn't mean…" Stopping mid-explanation, he stared down at her for a moment and then turned around and strode with quick steps out of the room.

Chapter 15

The moment his fingers had touched Callie's cheek, Landon felt a surge of electricity run through him; the intensity of which had shocked him so much that he immediately stood up and retreated quickly out of the room and into the quiet of his bedroom. But now as he sat on the edge of his bed, a wave of embarrassment rushed through him.

Shaking his head, he stared at his reflection in the full-length mirror hanging behind the bedroom door. "She must think you are insane. Why did you do that? She was being kind and you made it weird by touching her." As he was sitting slumped on his bed, annoyed and muttering to himself he heard footsteps in the hallway outside his room.

"Landon, are you okay?" The sweet sound of Callie's voice floating through the door prompted his heart to beat wildly against his chest. Her words were gentle as they touched his ears, and hearing them flushed him with even more embarrassment.

Taking a deep breath, he stood up, plastered a smile across his lips and strode to the door, opening it slowly. "I'm good, Callie. And I'm sorry about that."

Her lips curled into a gentle smile in response and as his eyes landed on her, he was struck again by how beautiful she was. She was wearing very little make-up and her red curls were loose and messy as they cascaded against her shoulders. And as she stood in the dimly lit hallway of his family's cabin, she took his breath away. And for the second time in ten minutes, he had the urge to place his lips against hers. He resisted that urge and instead, curled his lips into an apologetic smile. "I didn't mean to…"

She quickly shook her head, biting her bottom lip as she did and that tiny action on her part almost made Landon become unglued. He gripped onto the door as tightly as he could to keep himself from grabbing her. "It's all good, Landon. As long as we're good. I hope I didn't say anything to offend you."

Landon felt a slight punch to his stomach as her words touched his ears. He shook his head emphatically in response. "No, of course not. That was all me. I really am sorry. I just…"

As his voice trailed off, he watched as a glint of understanding flashed in her eyes and her lips curl upwards as a pink hue crept onto her cheeks. Her voice was gentle when she quietly responded. "Okay. Well, as long as we're good, then I guess I should go to bed." She turned around to leave and as she did, Landon reached out and placed his hand on her shoulder, not wanting her to leave just yet. She slowly turned around, turning wide eyes on him. "Landon?"

His name sounded so sweet as it touched his ears that he felt his knees weaken, prompting him to lean against the door frame. As he did, he dropped his hand from her shoulder, and nodded. A lump had formed in his throat and he had to clear it before he was able to respond. "Yeah, I, um, just thought maybe you wanted to watch a movie with me?" As he spoke, his lips trembled slightly and he wondered if she could see it. His eyes locked on to hers as he waited for her response and within seconds a twinkle danced across her eyes.

"Yeah, I'd like that."

Her answer filled him with joy and he beamed down at her and then followed as she led the way back to the living room. They plunked down, side by side on the couch, leaving a few inches of air between them and then started to surf through the Christmas movie selections on the TV guide.

As the remote highlighted, 'A Christmas Story', Landon's eyes lit up. "I love this movie."

"I've never seen it."

His eyes widened at her confession as she smiled shyly up at him, a hint of embarrassment shimmering in her eyes.

"Really?" Shock enveloped the single word as it left his lips, prompting her cheeks to darken as she released an embarrassed giggle and shrank a little into the couch cushions.

"Really!"

Landon shook his head while his lips curled upwards. "Well, I guess we know what we're watching." He then lifted himself up from the couch and grinned down at her. "I'll go get the popcorn."

She quickly jumped up beside him with a wide grin spread across her lips. "I'll make the hot chocolate."

He nodded, his grin matching hers as he led her into the kitchen. They worked as quietly as they could, not wanting to disturb the rest of the family and when their snacks were ready, they traipsed quietly back to the living room. As they watched the movie, Landon occasionally commented on a scene as they laughed and enjoyed their treats.

When the movie ended, Callie was grinning from ear to ear as she beamed brightly up at him. "That was a great movie. Thank you for choosing it."

He bowed slightly in his seat. "My pleasure, Miss Anderson!"

Her eyes sparkled as she giggled and laughter shook his shoulders as well. Leaning back against the couch, he took a sip of his hot chocolate and then turned a questioning glance in her direction. "So, are you ready for skating at the pond tomorrow?"

The moment the question left his lips, Callie groaned and the sparkle disappeared from her eyes. "Oh god! I almost forgot about that."

"What? You don't like skating?"

A tinge of red nestled upon her cheeks and a hint of discomfort flashed in her eyes. "Actually, I don't know how. I never learned. I was going to feign an illness in the morning to get out of it."

Landon's eyes grew wide again as her second confession of the night touched his ears. "Really? Even as a kid, you never skated?"

Shaking her head, he could see her discomfort growing as she shifted in her seat, which prompted him to touch her arm gently and lock his eyes onto hers. "I'm sorry, I don't mean to embarrass you. I just, I guess I was just curious. Skating was such a big part of our lives growing up, I sometimes forget that it may not have been for others."

Callie glanced down at his hand touching her and then let her eyes slowly move back up to his. "It's okay, you don't have to apologize but to answer your question, no, I've never been on the ice. Pops, well, let's just say that he was definitely not a skater and it never occurred to me to ask him to take me. Even in school, when we had the chance to skate, I didn't." She shook her head and turned her eyes away from him. "I'm not sure why. I guess I was always more interested in working with my hands than any kind of sports."

Landon nodded. "Well, I can teach you, if you want?" At his invitation, she glanced back up at him before turning her eyes down to stare at her lap. He knew she was trying to hide the red glow that was forming on her cheeks, so he placed a finger under her chin and brought her eyes back up to meet his gaze. "Callie, you don't have to be embarrassed. No one is going to judge you, I promise. Let me teach you. You have no idea how much fun you've been missing out on."

"I don't know. I mean, wouldn't you rather be on the ice enjoying yourself?"

"I would be enjoying myself. And besides, it's the least I can do after what you did for Scarlet tonight."

Callie tried to dip her head again, but his finger was still holding her chin up, so instead, she just shook her head. "I didn't do anything Landon. All I did was read a story."

"Callie..." Gentleness enveloped his voice as he gazed down at her with warm, soft eyes. "You did more than that and I'm grateful."

Her lips curled upwards at his response and she shrugged her shoulders. "Well, in that case. You're welcome. But you know, it really was my pleasure. You have an amazing daughter."

A bright smile touched Landon's lips and his eyes began to sparkle as he thought about his pride and joy.

"Thanks. I don't know how I got so lucky."

Callie grinned. "I do. It's because you, Officer Pierce, are a good father."

"Thank you, but sometimes I'm not so sure about that." As his confession exited his mouth, he heard the despair surrounding his voice and even though he wanted to, he couldn't hide it, as negative thoughts suddenly began to circle around his mind.

The grin immediately disappeared from Callie's lips. "Landon..."

Shaking his head, he offered her an apologetic smile. "I'm sorry, Callie. I didn't mean to get gloomy on you."

"Landon..."

He shook his head again and his lips curled upwards as he watched curiosity mixed with sadness cross her features. "It's okay, Callie. I'm okay."

"I don't think you are."

Sighing, he stood up and strolled to the window, knowing she was right. Stars were glittering in the night sky as he stared out at them. He heard Callie's footsteps come up behind him, but before she could say anything, he found himself confiding in her for the second time.

"I am okay, most of the time. It's just that ever since that dark, rainy October day four years ago when we stood at Izzie's grave and Scarlet blew her mother that one final kiss, I've worried that I'm not enough. I know she needs a mother and the older she gets, the more I worry that I'm not going to be able to fill that void."

Resting his eyes on Callie, he saw compassion filling her eyes. She placed her hand on his arm which was folded across his chest but she didn't speak, she just kept her soft gaze focused on him, prompting him to continue. "I know she has my mom and my sisters and they love her and I know that they will do anything for her but she needs a mom and I'm afraid that one day she's going to resent that I'm here and her mother isn't."

A gasp escaped Callie's throat at his confession. "Landon, I don't think…"

He quickly interrupted her before she could finish. "Did you? Ever resent your grandfather?"

Her response was immediate and her voice was full of conviction as she shook her head and locked her eyes onto his. "Never. Not once. I mean, yeah, I was sad that I didn't have a mom. But Pops was my life. He taught me everything I know and even as a kid, I knew how lucky I was to have him."

Landon's eyes held a hint of skepticism as they stared down at her. "What about when you saw all your friends with their mothers?"

Callie lifted her hands up and placed one on each of his cheeks, staring deeply into his eyes. "No, not even then. I never, ever resented my grandfather. He was my life Landon, just like you are for Scarlet. I know Scarlet misses her mother, I still miss mine everyday, but she will never resent that you are here and her mother isn't. I can see how much she loves you. And I know I've only known you both for a couple days but I do know that."

Tears glimmered in his eyes and slowly slid down his cheeks as a soft smile touched his lips. "Thank you,

Callie. I think I needed to hear that."

Dropping her hands from his cheeks, she offered him a reassuring smile. "You're welcome, Landon. I hope you really did hear me."

He grinned. "I did. It's just..." He let his voice trail off and she finished his sentence for him.

"Hard."

He nodded. "Yeah."

"I know but you're doing an amazing job with Scarlet. I know I'm not a parent but trust me, as someone who grew up with a single, male parent, you are doing better than you think and better than some people will ever do."

Landon smiled and then they dropped the subject after that and with silence surrounding them, began cleaning up their snack mess, before making their way upstairs to their separate bedrooms.

Landon laid in his bed that night, staring at his ceiling for a long time, thinking about their conversation and about Callie. And even though he didn't know it, she was laying under the warm covers in her own bed, thinking about him as well.

Chapter 16

Callie woke up the next morning after thinking about Landon for most of the night, with an annoying, persistent thought rolling around in her mind; it was annoying because she couldn't quite pin down what the thought was. But she felt like it was something that she was missing, something important. As she stared up at the ceiling, her mind rolled over her conversation with Landon from the previous night and as it did, she bolted up in her bed as her eyes widened with recollection. "That dark, rainy October day four years ago". She repeated Landon's words as disbelief began to swarm her. "No, it couldn't be; the mourners at the cemetery, it couldn't have been them." Grabbing her phone from the table beside her bed, she quickly typed, 'Izzie Pierce Obituary' onto the screen. As she waited for her phone to display the results of her search, Callie felt a knot in her stomach as the memory of that morning, four years ago, flashed through her mind; she still remembered the man and the little girl so clearly as well as the ache she had felt for them both. When the results popped up on the screen, she touched the first one, focusing her eyes on the tiny words that scrolled across the screen and as she read, her heart stopped for a second and a gasp escaped her lips.

"October tenth. Oh my god, it *was* them." Tears filled her eyes as the heart ache she had felt that day came flooding back and she started to feel it all over again. Leaning back against her headboard, she closed her eyes and tried to control her emotions as her mind wandered back to that gray, rainy day and the darkly-clad mourners, she had watched wiping away their tears. She recalled standing in pained silence as the young girl blew a kiss to the open grave. Tears slipped down Callie's cheeks as that memory flooded her mind. Turning her gaze to the window, she stared at the beauty outside and pondered what she should do with this sudden realization

"There's no point in saying anything. That would be weird, I mean what would you say? 'Oh, by the way Landon, I watched you at the cemetery when you were burying your wife'." She shook her head. "No, that would be weird and it doesn't matter. It was just a coincidence, lots of people are buried in that cemetery and besides, bringing it up would just make him sad." Nodding her head to confirm her decision, to keep this knowledge to herself, she climbed out of bed and stared out at the amazing view from her bedroom window, before strolling into her bathroom. As she showered, she tried to put her new realization out of her mind, but that was easier said than done, as the sadness of that day four years ago continued to envelop itself around her.

After allowing herself an extra long shower to rid the memories from her mind, she headed downstairs as the smell of bacon infiltrated her nostrils. The moment her slippered foot touched the last step of the stairs in the kitchen, her eyes landed on Landon. He was the only person in the room and he was standing at the stove with his back to her, humming 'Here comes Santa Claus', while swaying his body to the music. She stood for a moment, leaning against the wall watching him, with sadness surrounding her. But as she watched him moving happily to his own music, the happiness of the present pushed away the sadness of the past and a smile touched the corners of her eyes. After a few minutes of watching him and allowing his obvious joy to envelope her, she cleared her throat, immediately drawing his attention towards her.

The moment he turned around, Callie noticed a red hue creep from his neck onto his cheeks as he offered her a sheepish grin. "Callie. How long have you been standing there?"

Laughter danced in her eyes and her lips curled upwards to reveal a wide, mischievous grin. "Long enough to see your sweet dance moves."

The red hue turned a dark shade of crimson as he turned back to the pan on the stove. "Well, for that, missy, I don't think I'm gonna share any of this delicious bacon with you." He turned around to face her again and she could see he was trying to be serious but his voice held a hint of amusement and laughter sparkled in his eyes.

She set innocent eyes on him while offering him her sweetest smile. "I'm sorry, Officer. I think your dance moves are fantastic!" Her voice was sweet with a hint of amusement and Landon rolled his eyes while trying not to grin.

"Yeah, nice try! I know you're just saying that to get some bacon."

"Well, that bacon does smell pretty good. But Landon, I really was enjoying your performance, *a lot*." Her emphasis on the words 'a lot', prompted a loud groan to be let loose through Landon's lips.

Giggling at his embarrassment, she stepped further into the kitchen, and leaned against the counter, across from where he was working. After glancing around her, she focused curious eyes on him. "Where is everyone? It's awfully quiet in here."

Landon lifted his eyes to meet her gaze with an amused grin touching his lips. "Yeah, it's nice, isn't it?" Laughter shook her body, as he continued. "Mom and dad took the kids to the resort, it's the annual Santa pancake breakfast. They do it every year and they love

145

it. Even Jordie went."

Callie raised an impressed eyebrow. "Wow! That's pretty impressive."

His eyes danced as he nodded in agreement. "That's what we thought."

"What about Jade and Elliott and Mike and Tasha?"

Grabbing two plates from the cupboard beside him, Landon began loading bacon and eggs onto them as he answered. "Jade and Elliott went skiing and Mike and Tash took the ski doo's out for a ride." When he handed her a plate, she smiled her appreciation and then followed him to the table.

"Hmmm…so interesting. Looks like you and I have been paired up again."

Landon's eyes flew up to meet hers, a dash of surprise flickering within them. "What?"

Rolling her eyes, she chuckled. "Tell me you haven't noticed?"

The surprise in his eyes quickly turned to amusement. "I have. I just didn't think you had. Or at least I hoped you hadn't."

Laughter shook her whole body as she bit down on her fork, grinning up at him as she did. "That's good!"

"Thank you." Pride filled his eyes and a smile touched his lips.

"You're welcome and to answer you, yes, of course I've noticed. They haven't exactly been subtle about it, have they?"

Landon's shoulders shook with laughter. "No, they haven't." Pausing, he locked his eyes onto hers, staring at her softly. "But I haven't really minded."

Her lips curled into a gentle smile as she shook her head. "Neither have I."

Her response triggered joy to fill his eyes. "Well, in that case, Miss Anderson, how would you like to join me for a little shopping in the village?"

"Village?" Curiosity clouded her eyes as she stared at him across the table.

"Yeah. There's a village centered around the resort at the top of the mountain. Some great shops and there's this awesome little bakery, we could grab some dessert for after skating."

Her eyes had lit up at his description of the village but the moment he mentioned skating, she groaned and her eyes began to droop. "Oh my god! Don't remind me."

Her tone prompted a chuckle to escape Landon's throat, before he set understanding eyes on her. "I'm sorry. But you know, Callie. You don't have to go skating if you don't want to. I don't want to force you."

Shaking her head, she offered him a soft smile. "No, you aren't forcing me, Landon. I know you're right, I should try it at least once, it's just…I don't want to embarrass myself in front of everyone."

He nodded and then, she watched as an idea slowly grew in his eyes. "I have an idea."

"Okay?" Her response was tentative as uncertainty

filled her stomach.

"There's a skating rink in the village, it's not where we're going skating later, but, after we wander around the village, we can go there and I can show you the basics. Maybe help you feel more comfortable and less nervous when the rest of the family is around."

Surprise enveloped her as she lifted her eyes up to meet his. "Really? You would do that?"

"Of course." His eyes were twinkling with his response.

Callie was quiet as she thought about his suggestion and as she did, the dread within her slowly began to fade. Nodding slowly, she offered him an appreciative smile. "Okay. If you don't mind. I think I'd like that."

The twinkle began to dance across his eyes. "Good. Now let's finish breaky and then we can head up to the village."

Callie nodded, her eyes smiling as she shoveled a fork full of egg into her mouth. And then after quickly cleaning up the kitchen and getting ready, they were sitting in his SUV, on the way to the top of the mountain. It wasn't a long drive, but as Landon had explained, it was straight up hill and neither of them felt like doing that climb on foot. He found a parking spot in the large lot at the first entrance into the village and as they started strolling along the brick pathway leading to the village, she felt his gaze on her.

"So, I've been wondering something?"

Turning her attention to him, she could see curiosity enveloping his eyes as she questioned him. "What?"

"What's the story with the Impala? I mean, I'm guessing there's a story. It's a classic and not a very common one at that."

A sparkle touched Callie's eyes as a smile spread across her lips. She shook her head as she answered. "No, it isn't. And yes, there is a story. Pops and I fixed it up together."

His dark eyes grew wide as she watched a flicker of awe flood through them, prompting a flood of pride to rush through her body. "Wow!"

"Yup. But to be honest, it was mostly Pops. He started it before I was even born and then after mom died and grams got sick, he stopped working on it. We started working on it together when I was fifteen and finished it just before my seventeenth birthday." Nostalgia filled her eyes as she turned her them down and stared at the pathway underneath her feet, thinking about that time with her grandfather.

"That's amazing Callie."

Returning her gaze up to his, she was greeted by his perfect smile and eyes full of admiration. "Thanks. I think so too. And every time I crawl into it, I feel Pops around me." He nodded and they exchanged a smile before turning their focus to the village as it came into view. "Wow!" Callie's voice was full of wonder as her wide, brown eyes took in the sight in front of her. The Village looked like a village on a Christmas card. The sidewalks were cobblestone underneath a light layer of snow which was just starting to fall from the white clouds high above them. Snow-covered trees, decorated with colourful lights and decorations, lined the edges of the two-lane road. There was no sign of car traffic, only foot traffic as people milled through the streets and Christmas decorations adorned every window of every shop they passed. Callie's eyes remained wide as she moved her head from side to side trying to see everything at once. When her eyes eventually landed on Landon, he was grinning happily down at her.

"You like?"

She nodded slowly as a smile danced in her eyes. "This place is amazing. It's like a Christmas Village from the movies. I love it!"

Landon nodded as he beamed down at her. They spent the next two hours cruising in and out of shops, and Callie found some great souvenirs and gifts for herself and for her gracious hosts. The two of them talked and laughed and enjoyed their time roaming around the Village until they came upon the skating rink that Landon had mentioned earlier. In her enjoyment, Callie had forgotten about this part of the trip but once she laid her eyes on the rink, she felt a knot begin to form in her stomach. Glancing up at Landon, she knew her eyes were cloaked in dismay.

The moment his gaze landed on her; concern creased his forehead. "You don't have to do this, if you don't want to."

She shook her head. "I want to. I'm just nervous. But like my Pops used to say, fear is what stops you from living your best life, so Callie don't ever let fear stop you!"

Landon's eyes lit up as the crease in his forehead slowly disappeared. "Your Pops was a wise man."

"He was. Or he was just a really good negotiator. Cause that's how he always got me to do things I didn't want to do." A twinkle danced in her eyes and Landon shook with laughter.

"Well, as I see it, either way, he was a wise man!"

She laughed and nodded. "Yeah, I guess he was." She then glanced out at the rink full of people before turning her focus back on him. She straightened her shoulders, puffing her chest out, trying to show confidence she didn't quite have. "Okay, let's do this."

His lips curled upwards and then he strolled towards the rental hut as she followed close behind. After securing their purchases in a locker and securing their skates on their feet, there was nothing left to do but step out onto the ice. Callie took a deep breath as she stood up. Her legs were wobbly underneath her, prompting her to grab Landon's hand for support.

"Are you okay?" Concern dotted his eyes as he glanced down at her.

She nodded but didn't look up. She was using all of her concentration and strength to keep herself from falling flat on her butt. "I think so." Then, without waiting for him to respond, she took tentative steps towards the ice with him stepping in line with her. When they reached the entrance to the rink, she took another deep breath.

"It's okay. We can just take our time. Once you're on the ice, all you have to do is glide your feet. I'll help hold you up."

She nodded again, still not meeting his gaze; she was too busy concentrating on the ice in front of her. With one more deep breath, she stepped out onto the ice and although she was wobbly, she managed to do what he said and glide her feet along the surface. They moved slowly, making their way around the perimeter of the rink, staying close to the edge in an effort to avoid other skaters. Callie guessed that the rink was about half the size of an NHL rink, and after they had skated around the entire rink once, she glanced up at him with a look of victory shimmering in her eyes.

"I did it!"

Landon's eyes sparkled as he smiled down at her as delight enveloped his words. "You did. Shall we go again?"

She nodded enthusiastically, as she stared up at him with pink cheeks. "Yes, please! I kind of enjoyed that."

He laughed at her choice of words and then tightened his grip on her hand and led her around the rink again, she wobbled on occasion but he was right beside her, keeping her on her feet, each time.

They skated for almost an hour and by the time they took their skates off, Callie was exhausted but proud. She had skated around the rink without his assistance once and although she was slow, she managed to stay on her feet the entire time. As the two of them walked back through the Village to his SUV, Landon glanced at her with pride filled eyes.

"You did great out there!"

Callie's eyes landed on him and her lips curled upwards. Her eyes were warm and also full of pride. "Thanks, but it's only because I had a good teacher."

He scoffed, shaking his head. "No way, that was all you."

She giggled and shook her own head as they quietly made their way to the parking lot.

Later that afternoon, when it was time to join the entire family for the Pierce Family Skate, the nerves that Callie had been feeling earlier didn't reappear. Instead, a feeling of joy mixed with excitement filled her veins at the prospect of another family event. And the moment Landon grabbed her mitten covered hand with his own glove laden hand and the two of them glided around the ice, Callie felt that excitement shoot through her entire body. She skated with Landon and Jade and Scarlet and by the end of the night, everyone was amazed that she had only learned to skate that morning. She was sure they were all just being polite but she didn't care. She was happy and that was all that mattered when she crawled under her warm comforter that night and fell asleep dreaming about her day with Landon, the memories of that day in the cemetery, four years ago completely lost in the back of her mind.

Chapter 17

As Callie was falling asleep in her bed, Landon was laying in his own bed, unable to sleep as thoughts of her whirled through his mind. He had been right the other day; that he hadn't been this comfortable with a woman, with anyone really, since his late wife. Staring up at the ceiling with that realization in his head, Landon found himself starting to compare Callie to Izzie and the moment he did, he threw his covers aside, jumped up, pulled a t-shirt over his bare chest and wandered downstairs. After shrugging into his warm parka, he stepped into the cool, crisp night air, letting out a loud sigh as he plopped heavily down onto the swing. He was so wrapped up in his thoughts that he didn't realize that someone had followed him outside until a voice penetrated his ears.

"That was quite a sigh."

His heart jumped and so did he as he whirled his head around. A sheepish smile touched his lips when his eyes landed on Tasha. "Geez, Tash, you startled me."

A giggle escaped Tasha's throat as she made her way towards the swing and plopped down beside him. Her cheeks were red but since she was bundled up in a warm winter coat, he figured her red cheeks had more to do with the Bailey's, he had seen her pouring into her hot chocolate earlier that evening than the chilly night air.

"Thought you'd be upstairs, keeping Mike company." The smirk that formed at the corners of his mouth and the wink he gave her, provoked a slap that landed heavily against his jacket covered chest. "Ouch.

You're strong when you're drunk."

Tasha rolled her eyes but a mischievous smile touched the corners of her eyes. "Yeah, well you deserved that. Stop being gross."

A laugh slipped through Landon's lips and Tasha's shoulders shook with gentle laughter. But within seconds, the laughter left her body and she stared at him with concern resting across her features. "In all seriousness though, what's going on with you?"

His forehead creased as his eyebrows raised in question. "What do you mean?"

She sighed and tilted her head while giving him a 'you know exactly what I mean' look. "Lan…"

Shaking his head, he let his gaze fall to the dark night in front of them. "Nothing's going on with me. I'm just enjoying this fresh mountain air and the beautiful midnight view."

His response elicited a scoff to break out from Tasha's lips. "Yeah right."

"Yeah right, what?"

She leaned back against the swing as it moved slowly underneath them. "Do I really need to spell it out for you, big brother?" He tilted his head in question, but before he could reply, she continued. "That was no ordinary sigh. And if I'm not mistaken, it had Callie written all over it."

Landon shook his head, focusing his eyes back on his sister. "Oh, you think so, do you?"

She nodded. "We can all see it, Landon. The way

you look at her. The way she looks at you. All week, the two of you have laughed and talked like old friends and have been practically inseparable. And you and I both know it's not just because mom and Jade keep pairing you up. There's a connection there and don't even try to deny it."

Leaning back against the swing, Landon let out another long sigh. "I didn't think anyone had noticed."

Laughter shook Tasha's body as she shook her head. "It's been pretty hard not to. None of us have seen you like this since…" Stopping mid-sentence her eyes widened and realization mixed with sympathy began to permeate her eyes. "Oh Landon…"

As he watched her eyes soften, Landon felt an ache in his heart as he thought about his late wife and then as he did, the pain of her affair washed over him, stabbing into his heart. He quickly diverted his gaze from his sister and focused it on the dark night around him. "Tasha, can we not have this conversation?"

"I think we have to."

"Why?" He could feel her eyes on him, but he kept his eyes focused on the world around him, instead of meeting her gaze.

"Because I want you to move on and I think you're stuck in the past, in the pain."

He sighed and felt his whole body begin to shrink in defeat as he turned his eyes to meet hers. His voice was enveloped in despair when he responded. "It's been four years. Don't you think that I should be ready to move on?"

Tasha shrugged. Her eyes were full of compassion

as she offered him a warm smile. "I don't know, Lan. But I don't think it's just about the guilt of moving on." Her words caught him off guard and a gasp slipped through his lips. But before he could question her, she answered his unasked question. "I know about the affair, Landon."

"What?" The word was shrill out of his mouth as her confession stopped his heart. "But how?"

"Izzie told me. Right before she died. She wasn't sure if you knew and neither was I. At least not until you saw that picture the other day. Your reaction confirmed it."

Standing up, Landon walked to the edge of the porch as confusion took over his mind. "But...I don't understand." He turned around and narrowed his confused eyes on his sister. "Why did she tell you? And why didn't you tell me?"

A tear shimmered in Tasha's eyes as she stood and walked towards him, stopping directly in front of him. As she shook her head, he could see a mixture of guilt and apology floating in her eyes. "I don't really know why she told me. I think she needed to confess it to someone before she left and she couldn't bare to tell you. You had been so amazing right until the end and your heart was already breaking. I don't think she wanted to add to that and honestly Landon, neither did I." Sincerity wrapped her words and without responding, he folded his arms around her and pulled her against his chest. She returned his embrace and they stood together for a long moment before Landon dropped his arms, allowing Tasha to step back. There were tears in his eyes as he stared down at her.

"Thank you, Tash. I'm sorry you had to live with that for so long."

She nodded. "And I'm really sorry I didn't tell you. I just wasn't sure if I should and…" Uncertainty and apology enveloped her words as he shook his head, stopping her before she could finish her apology.

"You did the right thing, Tash. Izzie confided in you and you honoured that. So, thank you."

"You're welcome." Her lips curled upwards then, as a sparkle shone in her eyes. "Okay, so, now that we've got that sorted out, let's get back to Callie."

A surprised laugh flew out of Landon's mouth. "Nice transition there, sis."

Tasha's eyes danced as she grinned up at him. "Hey, you know me. I've never been one to waste time."

He was grinning widely as he shook his head. "No, you definitely don't do that. But in all seriousness, I'm not sure what there is to say."

"Do you like her?"

Landon sighed but the grin remained spread across his lips. "I do. She's one of the most amazing people I've ever met. She's kind and charming and funny and sweet and she even laughs at my jokes."

Tasha grinned. "Well, in that case, I'd say she's a keeper."

He shook his head, while rolling his laughter-filled eyes. "Thanks for that, sis."

"You're welcome." A proud grin touched her lips as he rolled his eyes again. They laughed together for a moment until the laughter in Tasha's eyes disappeared.

"So, then, what's the problem, Lan? Because I can tell that she likes you too."

Shaking his head sadly as the laughter left his body, he sighed. "The problem, is that I'm…"

"Scared." She finished his thought for him and he nodded as apprehension crept across his face and landed in his eyes.

As she stared with sympathy into his eyes, she gently placed her hand on his shoulder and spoke with a firm but gentle tone. "I get that, Landon. I do. But Callie isn't Izzie. And I don't mean to speak ill of the dead but even on her best days, Izzie was all about Izzie." He opened his mouth to defend his wife, but Tasha put her hand up and shook her head. "Let me finish. Don't get me wrong, I loved Izzie and I miss her too. She was an amazing mother and person but when it came to you, she was selfish. I know you saw it and now that she's gone, you've forgotten it but it was always what Izzie wanted. But Callie, Callie's different. I know you can see it, and, I know that I don't know her well, but I do know that she's the kind of person who fixes someone's car in minus freezing weather and does it with a smile on her face. And she's the kind of person who gives you high fives and tells you that you did great even though you just bombed at charades." A smirk touched the corners of Tasha's mouth, then and Landon rolled his eyes as she continued. "Callie cares so much about others that I feel it in my heart that she wouldn't hurt you like that. And even if it doesn't work out with her, isn't it time for you to start thinking about Landon and let go of the hurt and guilt and all of it? Because I know that Izzie would want you to be happy. She would want you to live your life to the fullest. And all the best things and people in life are worth the risk, don't you think?"

Landon felt a tear slip down his cheek which he wiped away quickly before offering his sister a soft smile. His eyes peered down on her with all the love he felt for her. "You are a wise woman, little sis. Thank you."

Pride filled Tasha's eyes as she wrapped her arms around his neck and whispered in his ear. "You're welcome. Now, what are you going to do about it?"

His strong arms enveloped her and he squeezed her tightly while chuckling softly. "I guess I have some thinking to do."

As she pulled out of his arms, she had a twinkle sparkling in her eyes. "As long as that thinking leads back to Callie."

"Ha! Okay, young lady. Don't you have a man waiting for you upstairs?"

"Okay, fine, I'll go now. I love you, Landon."

"Love you too, Tash. Good night."

"Night." She turned around and skipped back into the house, leaving Landon alone in the quiet night to contemplate everything she had said and everything he was feeling. It didn't take him long to realize what he wanted and he only hoped that Tasha was right in her assessment about Callie's feelings too.

Chapter 18

The following morning, Callie was standing in the kitchen after breakfast staring at Jade with wide, shock-filled eyes. "A ball? Jade, are you kidding me? How are you just telling me now, about a Christmas Eve, Eve ball that we are supposed to attend tonight?" Disbelief encompassed Callie's words and swam in her eyes as she stared with her mouth gaped wide open at her friend.

Innocence filled Jade's eyes as she shrugged her shoulders. "I'm sorry, Callie. But I did tell you to bring something nice for New Year's so you can just wear that tonight."

Callie shook her head, huffing out a sigh as she did. "Why wouldn't you tell me about this sooner? A Christmas Eve, Eve ball sounds much fancier than a New Year's Eve party, Jade." Annoyance rang through Callie's words.

Jade grinned, ignorant to Callie's annoyance, as a twinkle sparkled in her eyes. "It isn't really. I'm sure whatever you brought will be great."

Callie rolled her eyes at her friend before storming upstairs to her bedroom in a huff. She slumped onto the edge of her bed and stared out the window, taking a moment to appreciate the view outside as she took a long, deep, calming breath. After several minutes, she strolled towards her closet to survey the limited number of clothing selections hanging within it.

And later that evening, after hours spent preparing her hair and make-up, Callie stood in front of the full-length mirror that hung on the back of her bedroom door, sighing at the reflection looking back at her.

"What have you gotten yourself into?" She moaned at the mirror as she fidgeted with the hem of the short, navy-blue dress. The dress was brand new, one she had purchased for this trip after Jade had told her about New Year's Eve. And now as she stared at herself, she was beginning to have buyers' remorse. The sleeveless dress itself, was beautiful, with lace trim across the sweetheart neckline, which clung to her chest and revealed just enough cleavage to make her feel the right amount of sexy. The dress hugged all the generous curves of her body perfectly and although she was happy with the dress itself, it was the short length of it, that was causing the remorse to rise up within her. As she was staring at her legs, trying to pull the hem down, there was a soft rap on her door and the moment she said come in, Jade popped into the room, looking stunning as usual and creating even more anxiety within Callie's heart.

Jade let out a loud whistle as her eyes roamed up and down Callie's body. As she stepped further into the room, Jade offered her a wide grin. "Wow, Callie. You are a knock out. That dress is amazing."

Glancing at her friend, Callie smiled weakly. She stood up straight as her eyes wandered back to the mirror. Jade came to stand behind her and they made eye contact through the mirror. Tilting her head, Callie raised an eyebrow. "You think?" Callie questioned Jade, but before Jade could respond, Callie shook her head and went back to playing with the hemline of her dress. "I don't know." Her lips curled downwards as she stared miserably at her reflection.

Jade leaned into Callie's back, resting her head on Callie's shoulder. "Callie, this dress is amazing on you. You look beautiful."

Callie's frown deepened as she looked through the

mirror at her friend and then back at herself. "You don't think it makes my legs look huge. I mean, I know I don't have the thinnest legs but…"

Jade's lips curled upwards and her eyes softened as she continued staring at Callie's reflection. "Your legs are perfect and so are you. Trust me. I think you look beautiful and I'm sure I'm not the only one who will think so."

The curl of Jade's lips turned into a smirk and she shot a wink in Callie's direction, prompting Callie to turn around and stare into her friend's eyes with a curious gaze. "Oh yeah and pray tell who else will think so?"

The smirk widened across Jade's lips, while her eyes twinkled brightly. "I think you know, exactly who I'm talking about. But I'll give you a hint, you and him have been inseparable since we got here."

Rolling her eyes as she shook her head, Callie grabbed her silver clutch purse and strolled towards the door. "Come on crazy lady. Let's get going."

Laughter shook Jade's body as she followed Callie out of the room. "You know I'm right."

Callie rolled her eyes again and responded over her shoulder. "Yeah, well, that's only because we're the only singles in the group. You all keep pairing up and that leaves just me and him. So, whatever you think is happening, isn't. It's just circumstance."

Jade laughed. "If you say so."

Callie sighed but didn't respond. Making her way downstairs with Jade behind her, Jade's comments swirled in her mind but when she saw Landon standing in the living room waiting with the rest of the group, she pushed them to the back of her mind; choosing to focus on the night ahead of her instead.

As the silver high heels that encased her feet touched the bottom of the staircase, her eyes focused on Landon as he turned towards her and his eyes grew wide. A smile spread across his lips and his eyes sparkled brightly as she made her way towards him. "Callie, you look stunning! That dress...wow!"

Watching his eyes wander down her body, Callie felt warmth flush her cheeks. Diverting her eyes down, she took a moment to slow her suddenly rapidly beating heart. When she brought her eyes back up to meet his, he was beaming down at her. "Thanks." She responded shyly as she took a moment to assess his choice of outfit. "You clean up pretty good yourself, Officer."

Looking down at himself, Landon laughed and then brought his eyes back up to meet hers. "Thanks. I usually hate dressing up, but mom insisted."

Callie laughed and then without meaning to, her eyes wandered back over his muscular body. The charcoal gray suit looked like it was tailored just for him as it clung to his toned body perfectly. As her eyes moved back upwards, they lingered on the blue and white striped tie hanging against his crisp, white dress shirt. She smiled as she met his gaze. "We match."

Landon's eyes widened slightly, prompting her to point to his tie. He glanced down, following her gesture and then quickly raised his sparkling eyes to meet hers. "So, we do. Good job us!"

She giggled at his comment and his shoulders shook with laughter but before they could continue their conversation, Courtney entered the room and began to shepherd them all out to the waiting cars. She had

166

ordered drivers for the evening so that everyone could enjoy themselves and not have to worry about getting back to the cabin. Callie and Landon strolled together out the front door and sat side by side in the first vehicle with Jade and Elliott in the seat in front of them. Her friend and her fiancé were busy discussing some wedding details as they drove up the mountain, leaving Callie and Landon to talk quietly with each other. Callie watched the snow-covered trees pass by her window for a moment before resting her gaze on Landon, whose eyes were focused on the world outside.

"So, tell me about where we're going tonight? Jade said it's the Christmas Eve, Eve Ball?"

Landon's lips curled upwards as he turned his focus to her. "Yeah. They hold it every year at the resort up the hill. And of course, it's one of the Pierce family Christmas traditions." Laughter danced in his eyes as the corners of Callie's mouth curved upwards.

"So, there will be dancing?"

"Absolutely." His smile curved into a smirk. "I hope you don't have two left feet."

Grinning, she shrugged her shoulders. "I don't really know. I don't think I've danced since high school and that was just line dancing in gym class."

Landon's mouth dropped open and he stared at her with wide, disbelieving eyes. "What? You didn't go to dances in high school? What about prom?"

She shook her head. "Nope. Never had anyone to go with. Most guys were intimidated by me."

Landon shook his head while warmly gazing down at her. "Well, most guys are stupid."

Their eyes locked and Callie felt a flutter dance through her body. Silence surrounded them for a moment before Landon's lips curled upwards and he broke the silence. "Well, don't worry. I'll teach you."

She grinned, as her eyes sparkled. "Oh, yeah? Officer Pierce dances?"

"I'll have you know, Miss Anderson, I am an excellent dancer." His words were cloaked in pride, prompting her grin to widen.

"I can't wait to see that." Their eyes locked again as another moment of silence enveloped them, but it wasn't long before Jade turned in her seat and interrupted that silence.

"We're here!" Jade's eyes were dancing wildly and the excitement in her voice was contagious as excitement enveloped Callie. She quickly turned to Landon with a bright, happy grin stretched across her lips.

"Hurry up, Officer. I can't wait to see your dance moves!" She pushed him lightly and he laughed while quickly climbing out of the car. Holding his hand out to assist her, his eyes sparkled when he beamed up at her.

"Let's go, m' lady!" As she grabbed his hand, he bowed prompting a fit of giggles to burst out of her mouth.

When they entered the beautiful resort, Callie felt excitement rush through her and the hairs on the back of her neck stood straight up. Looping her arm into Landon's, she allowed him to lead her into the ballroom, as she glanced around in awe; never had she seen anything so beautiful. Tiny white lights dangled from the high ceilings, setting off a soft glow in the otherwise dark room. Every table was adorned with a beautiful white bouquet of Lilies and Baby's Breath and the white table linens were accented with red runners. Several beautifully decorated Christmas trees adorned the outer perimeter of the room, giving one the feel of Christmas without being tacky. Callie found herself holding her breath in awe as Landon guided her to their table in the center of the room.

When they reached the table, he pulled a chair out and motioned for her to sit. "Your seat, m' lady."

Callie was still in awe of her surroundings as she turned wide eyes on him. She glanced down at the chair and then offered him an appreciative smile. "Thank you, kind sir."

He grinned and nodded as she sat down. After pushing her chair in, he took a seat beside her and she watched as the rest of his family took their seats around the table. Once everyone was seated, the conversation became lively but Callie found herself zoning out as she gazed around the room, watching the rest of the guests milling about around them. She was in awe of all the beautiful dresses and suits and was faintly aware of Christmas music playing softly in the back ground. And it wasn't until Landon touched her arm and his deep voice penetrated her mind that she noticed everyone else at the table had disappeared.

"Earth to Callie. Would you care to take that dance lesson now?"

Callie turned surprised eyes on him before quickly surveying the empty table. When her eyes found their way back to his, she offered him a slightly embarrassed, slightly apologetic smile. "Sorry, Landon.

I was just taking this all in. Where is everyone?"

Amusement touched his eyes as he smiled warmly down on her. "They all hit the dance floor." Offering her his hand, he tilted his head and raised an eyebrow in her direction. "Care to join them?"

Callie's eyes wandered from him to the dance floor across the room and then back to him. Nodding, she placed her hand in his. "Absolutely. But if I step on your toes, don't say I didn't warn you."

Laughter touched his eyes as he grinned widely. "I'll consider myself warned."

She smiled as he stood up, pulling her up with him and then he guided her out onto the dance floor. As he twirled her around and placed his hand on her waist, she felt a surge of electricity and excitement course through her body. Her heart began to race as she placed her hand on his shoulder, like she had seen the women do in countless movies. As Landon began to move, she followed his lead. She glanced around the dance floor before letting her attention focus back on him; he was staring down at her, a soft, warm smile touching his lips.

Her lips curled upwards as their eyes locked. "This isn't too hard."

He grinned and was about to respond when her foot landed hard on his. Her eyes widened as he grimaced but even as he did, their bodies continued to move together.

"Oh my gosh. Landon, I'm so sorry."

Shaking his head, he was about to respond when she stepped on his foot a second time. This time, she stopped moving entirely, bringing him to a stop with her. As she dropped her hand from his shoulder and stepped back, she looked at him with wide, apologetic eyes. "I'm sorry, Landon. Maybe we shouldn't do this. I don't want to hurt you."

Landon immediately shook his head, grabbed her hand and stepped towards her, bringing his arm back up to her waist. He pulled her close to him and began moving to the music again. As he did, she instinctively placed her hand back on his shoulder. His voice was gentle when he responded. "Don't be silly. You aren't hurting me. And you know what they say? Practice makes perfect."

She didn't respond, instead, she just nodded and then allowed him to lead her around the dance floor. Within minutes, she began to feel more comfortable in his arms and when they left the dance floor to grab a drink, she hadn't stepped on his foot again. Getting back to the table with their drinks in hand, they found Tasha and Mike and Courtney and Nick engrossed in conversation. When none of them noticed them sit down, Landon leaned in close to Callie's ear.

"Do you want to get some fresh air? The view from the terrace is amazing!"

Without responding, Callie stood up and Landon quickly followed her lead. She looped her hand into his arm and let him lead her across the ballroom to the French doors that led out onto the terrace. The moment she stepped across the threshold into the night air, a breeze whipped past her and although heaters had been placed strategically around the outer perimeter, she felt a shiver shoot down her back and the little pricks of goosebumps quickly sprang up onto her arms. She immediately wrapped her arms around her body, rubbing them as she did.

Within seconds, she heard Landon's voice beside her. "This was a dumb idea." She turned her gaze to him but before she could reply, he was draping his jacket over her shoulders.

She immediately shook her head. "I'm okay, Landon. Now, you'll be cold."

His eyes were gentle as he gazed down at her. "Don't worry about me. I'm fine." Turning his gaze away from her then, he stepped towards the railing of the terrace. "Come, you need to see this view."

Her lips curled upwards as she followed him. Coming to a stop right beside him, she felt her breath catch in her throat as she admired the snow-covered mountains that were laid out before them. The bright light of the nearly full moon shone down to create a shimmering effect on the snow-touched trees. Her eyes wandered further out into the night and she stood in awe of the beauty of nature in front of her. After a few moments of silence, she whispered into the night.

"Wow! I don't think I've ever seen anything so beautiful!"

"Me neither." Landon's response was also a faint whisper.

As her gaze took in the sights around her, she looked up into the clear night sky and smiled when her eyes fell on the millions of twinkling stars above them. "Wow! I thought the sky back home was beautiful but this…" She turned her eyes to Landon, who offered her a warm smile before turning his gaze towards the sky.

"Yes, it is…"

As she stood beside Landon in silence, staring up into the night, Callie felt an overwhelming sense of nostalgia sweep across her and a smile touched her lips as she began to speak quietly. "When I was young, my Grams used to tell me that my mom was up with the stars, shining down on me, watching me. And when Grams passed away, I would spend hours staring up at the stars, knowing that Grams and my mom were together. And now my Pops is up there with them and all three of them are shining down on me. And sometimes when I'm feeling lonely or sad, I sit outside on my back deck and stare up at the twinkling night sky and then, I don't feel as lonely because I know that the three of them are together, watching over me." She turned her mist clouded eyes towards him as she finished her story, and the moment she saw the look of sympathy surface in his eyes, she felt heat rise within her; embarrassment shooting through her body. Quickly wiping the tears that were forming through the mist, she offered him a sheepish grin. "I'm sorry, Landon. I didn't mean to darken the mood."

The sympathy quickly left Landon's eyes and was replaced with reassurance as he placed his hand gently on top of her hand, which was laying on the railing in front of her. She glanced down at their touching hands and felt warmth radiating from his touch. When she glanced back up at him, his dark gray eyes penetrated hers and he was shaking his head. "You didn't darken anything and I'm glad you shared that with me. I'm glad you have the stars to keep you company." As he spoke, his voice lowered and his eyes softened. "I don't want you to feel lonely, Callie." His soft eyes piercing hers caused her pulse to quicken and her heart to beat rapidly against her chest.

"I don't feel lonely, here with you." The words exited her mouth in a hushed whisper.

Their eyes remained locked together as Landon stepped closer to her until there was barely an inch of air between them.

"Callie…" Her name was a raspy whisper off his lips and as he spoke, he inched his face closer to hers.

She took in a sharp intake of breath in anticipation of what was coming next as excitement for this moment coursed through her body. Then, within seconds, his lips brushed up against hers. His lips were warm and she closed her eyes waiting for more but just as he pressed his lips against hers again, she heard a voice from behind her, cut through the quiet night.

"Oh, sorry you two, I didn't mean to interrupt. I, um…"

The moment Callie heard Jade's voice, her eyes snapped open and she spun around. She could feel heat rising within her again as she stared at the smirking face of her friend. Feeling Landon stiffen beside her, Callie turned towards him and she could see a pink hue darkening his cheeks as he stared at his sister.

He cleared his throat. "No worries, Jade. What's up?"

Jade's eyes glanced from Landon to Callie and back to Landon as the smirk widened across her lips and amusement framed her eyes. "Mom wants to get a group photo. Everyone's waiting by the stage."

Callie nodded as her gaze landed on Landon. He stared down at her and she could see disappointment flash in his eyes, prompting a flutter to dance across her heart. He offered her a smile before turning his attention back to his sister. "Okay, we're coming."

Jade grinned at them both and then turned on her heel, leaving Landon and Callie alone on the terrace. Landon's soft, gentle, sparkling eyes found hers as he held his hand out in front of him. "Shall we go? And continue this later?"

Callie felt a wave of joy wash over her as she nodded, smiling brightly up at him while placing her hand in his. His hand was warm as it wrapped around hers and Callie felt electricity spark through her body as he led her back into the ballroom to his waiting family. After numerous pictures were taken, Callie found herself back in Landon's arms on the dance floor. They danced and ate and laughed with his family and she was both exhausted and exhilarated when they made their way home well after midnight.

When everyone else made their way upstairs to bed, Callie and Landon stayed outside on the porch swing, watching the stars twinkling above them. Silence encompassed the night as they stared out into the darkness and it was Landon who eventually broke the silence between them.

"Callie about earlier…" She turned her eyes on him as a smile touched her lips. She didn't speak, waiting for him to continue. His eyes were sparkling down on her and she could see a hint of hope mixed with the tiniest hint of fear lingering within them. "I just wanted to say, I mean, I hope that wasn't, I hope you don't…I mean, I hope I wasn't overstepping."

Callie smiled at the awkwardness that surrounded him. Reaching up she placed her hand gently against his cheek and then as she stared softly into his eyes, she leaned forward, pressing her lips against his. Her touch was soft and tentative at first but he quickly sunk into her kiss and began moving his lips with hers. When she pulled away a few moments later, they were both smiling. "You weren't overstepping Landon."

His lips curled upwards and then he quickly placed his lips against hers again. Leaning towards him, Callie wrapped her hands around his neck and he placed his on the small of her back, pulling her body into his. Callie felt heat coursing through her, as their lips moved hungrily together. When they pulled apart a few minutes later, they were both smiling and breathless.

Landon reached up and tucked a red curl behind her ear and as he did his eyes, moved downwards and landed on the gold necklace that was dangling from her neck. He touched the chain, his hand brushing against her naked skin as he did, sending an electric shock down her spine. He then let his hand rest on her shoulder as he smiled down on her. "I've been meaning to ask you all night what the story is behind this necklace. I don't think I've seen it before."

Callie's hand instinctively touched the tiny 'J' that dangled from the chain as she smiled softly up at him. "It was my mother's. I wear it on special occasions to keep her with me."

Landon offered her a soft, appreciative smile as his eyes filled with curiosity. "What does the J stand for?"

Callie's eyes darted back down to the necklace. "Janet." As she lifted her eyes back up to meet his, a moment later, she noticed that the colour had drained from his face and his eyes were wide as they stared down at her.

"Janet. As in Janet Anderson?"

Callie nodded as a feeling of dread began to replace the happiness in her heart. "Yeah, why? Landon, you look like you've seen a ghost, what's going on?"

Landon jumped up from the swing and began pacing across the porch. After a few paces, he stopped and stared down at her. "Callie, you said your mother died in an accident. What happened?"

Standing up, Callie shook her head. "Landon, what's going on?" Uncertainty and fear enveloped her voice as she tried to understand the sudden change in his behaviour.

"Callie, please, just tell me."

"Well, my mom was an addict and had been for years. She got sober when she was pregnant but it wasn't long after I was born that she reverted back to her old ways. One night she got high and stumbled out onto the road and was hit by a car. Pops told me that it was an accident, that it was a really dark, rainy night and the driver of the car didn't see her until it was too late."

Callie watched as Landon took a step back. Fear was filling his eyes as he shook his head. "Callie, when did this happen? What was the date?"

She shook her head as confusion rocked through her body. "Landon, what..."

"Callie, was November eighteen, twenty-two years ago?"

Callie's eyes grew wide and the dread boiling within her formed a knot in her stomach. "Landon, how do you know that?"

The fear in his eyes turned to misery and he shook his head while staring down at her with streams of tears running down his cheeks. "It was me, Callie. I was the driver. The accident I told you about, was the one that killed your mother. I did it. I was driving that car."

Callie felt like she had been punched in the stomach as she stared up at him. She wobbled and then landed hard on the swing, feeling light headed as she stared up at him in disbelief. "I don't understand..."

He shook his head in despair. "I'm so sorry Callie." The words were enveloped in remorse and tears and before she could respond, he marched towards the door and disappeared into the cabin, leaving her alone on the porch, completely gutted by the confession he had just dropped on her.

Chapter 19

Storming into the cabin with a heavy heart, Landon couldn't believe what had just transpired. As the memory of that night twenty-two years ago flashed through his mind, he felt misery and pain envelope his entire being. As his legs guided him towards the kitchen, he stopped abruptly when he came face to face with his parents, who were sitting in their bathrobes at the kitchen table holding tea cups in their hands.

The smile on his mother's face evaporated the moment her eyes landed on him. "Landon, honey, what happened?"

His stomach tightened into a knot as he stared at his parents. The look of concern on his mother's face was mirrored by his father and Landon felt like his whole world was collapsing around him. Shaking his head, he slumped into the chair beside his father just as his knees gave out underneath him. Misery circled his eyes and enveloped his words when he muttered quietly. "Janet Anderson." As soon as her name left his lips, he watched a shadow of memory and sadness creep into the eyes of both his parents.

His father was the first to speak; his voice was quiet and enveloped in dark memories. "What about her son?"

Landon's dark eyes filled with pain as he met his father's gaze. "She was Callie's mother."

A gasp escaped his mother's lips as his father's jaw dropped. Shaking his head, his father stared at him in disbelief. "Are you sure? How do you know?"

"Callie just told me."

His mother's eyes widened. "She knew?"

Landon shook his head. "No." Agony encased his words. "Not until I told her."

Confusion began to dot his father's eyes and crease his forehead. "But how did you know?"

Landon closed his eyes and let out a long, deep sigh. When he reopened them, both his parents were staring at him with anticipation. He shook his head in misery as he began his story. "I'm not sure if you noticed the necklace she was wearing tonight, it had the letter J dangling from it. I was curious, so I asked her about it. Apparently, it was her mothers and she wears it on special occasions, to feel close to her mom. And when I asked what her mother's name was, she told me...Janet."

Sympathy mixed with shock, clouded his mother's eyes. "Landon..."

"I know mom..." Tears slipped down his cheeks and as they did, his mother stood up from her seat and wrapped her arms around his neck. He immediately folded his arms around her and buried his face into her neck. His body shuddered as the memory of the accident flooded his mind. He let himself lean into his mother's embrace, allowing her comfort to envelope him. They held each other for a long time before she returned to her seat. When she did, Landon watched as his parents exchanged a glance and grabbed onto each other's hands. He knew this moment was as difficult for them as it was for him. "I'm sorry that I brought this all up again." His voice was grim as he glanced between the two of them with misery-soaked eyes.

His father was quick to shake his head. "Don't be sorry, son. It wasn't your fault then and it isn't your fault now."

"Tell that to Callie."

"What did she say when you told her?" His mother's question was soft and enveloped in concern.

Landon shook his head. "Nothing. I told her and then came inside."

His mother's forehead creased with concern. "Landon, you left her alone after hearing that?"

The misery returned to his eyes. "Mom, I wasn't sure what to do. I just confessed to killing her mother. What was I supposed to say after that?" He shook his head miserably. "But you're right, she probably shouldn't be alone. Can you?"

She nodded as she stood up and without another word, slipped out of the kitchen. Both Landon and his father watched her go and then Landon sensed his father's gaze land back on him.

"Are you okay son? I know that you and Callie were getting close."

The memory of her lips on his flashed through Landon's mind, prompting the knot in his stomach to tighten even more. He turned anguished eyes towards his father as his head drooped in misery. "Yeah, you could say that, dad. But now, none of that matters. Whatever we had or could have had is over."

"How do you know that, son? Did Callie say that?"

"No, but how could it not be? How could she feel

anything but anger towards me now?"

"Son, Callie doesn't strike me as an irrational woman. She must know that it was an accident."

"She does, but..."

His father shook his head and was about to reply when his mother rushed back into the room, drawing the attention of both men. "Callie wasn't outside. She must have gone up to her room."

Landon shook his head before dropping his chin against his chest; the emotions of everything that had happened that night swirling in his mind. When he looked up at his parents, his father was staring at him.

"Go talk to her, Landon. If you think she's worth fighting for, go fight for her."

Landon glanced from his father to his mother and then stood up. He wasn't sure if going to her was the right decision but he knew that she was worth fighting for, so he marched upstairs, fighting to keep his fears and insecurities from swallowing him as he went. When he arrived at her bedroom door, he took a deep breath and just as he was raising his hand to knock, the sound of crying floated through the door. The sound hit him hard and his stomach dropped. Pain and sorrow circled his heart with the knowledge that he was the cause of her tears and pain. Lowering his hand, he stood quietly outside her door, contemplating his next move.

Chapter 20

When Callie was able to compose herself enough to stand, after Landon had left her stunned and alone on the porch, she opened the front door and let out a sigh of relief when her eyes confirmed that the coast was clear. Tiptoeing up the stairs, with tears cascading down her cheeks, she held her breath, praying that she didn't run into anyone in the hallway. She wasn't sure she would be able to speak if she did, let alone explain the tears that were tumbling from her eyes. When she made it to the sanctuary of her bedroom, she closed the door and slumped against it, allowing gravity to pull her to the floor. As she rested her head on her knees, loud sobs began to escape her throat and shake her body. She tried to control them, but they were beyond control, so she wrapped her hands around her knees and let the waterfall of tears puddle onto the floor beneath her.

As she huddled on the floor, her heart aching as she allowed herself to feel all of her emotions, she heard a soft rap against the door behind her. Closing her mouth to silence her sobs, she instinctively wiped the tears from her eyes but didn't respond. After a moment of silence, Landon's soft voice permeated through the door, touching her ears and increasing the ache in her heart.

"Callie, it's Landon. I know you're upset but can we talk? Please?"

Continuing to wipe the tears that were slipping down her cheeks, Callie took a deep breath before rising and slowly opening the door. She knew her face was red and puffy and conveyed all of the ache and sadness she was feeling and staring at Landon, she saw the same ache and sadness mirrored in his blood-shot eyes. Shaking her head, she swallowed the lump of tears in her throat before speaking softly. "Landon, I don't think…"

"Callie, I know you're upset and I understand if you hate me but I really need…"

Holding her hand up, she stopped him mid-sentence. "Landon, I can't. Not right now. I need time to think." Tears enveloped her words and as she watched fear and anguish fill his eyes, she felt her whole body weaken with emotion, forcing her to lean against the door frame.

He wiped away the tear that was slipping down his cheek as he stared at her, nodding his head. "I know and I get that but I'm afraid that if we don't talk now, we won't be able to find our way back."

Callie shook her head again and her voice cracked with defeat when she spoke. "Back to what Landon? We barely know each other and you just told me that you were the one driving the car that killed my mother. That day changed my whole life. You changed my whole life. I need time to digest that. To figure out what that means for me. I need to figure out how I live with that, if I can."

He nodded again as his shoulders began to sag and his head drooped; defeat and regret washing across his features. His voice was hoarse but quiet when he responded. "Okay. You're right. I am responsible for all of it. But I need you to know that I'm sorry and that I wish things had been different." He locked his eyes on to hers before turning on his heel and swiftly walking to his own bedroom. She stood in her doorway and watched as he disappeared without looking back. When the hallway was empty, she closed her door, resting her head against it. The memories of their week together began to flood her mind, cracking her already broken heart. The ache in her heart grew as she thought about her mother and about the man, the boy who had been behind the wheel that fateful night. Turning around, she glanced at the night stand beside her bed, her eyes landing on the journal that she had been writing in, on and off, for the past three years. She crossed the room with three long strides, snatched it up and flipped to the page that read November eighteen two thousand nineteen. Sinking onto the bed, she read the words that she had written two years ago; the twentieth anniversary of her mother's death.

Chapter 21

Christmas Eve morning dawned bleak for Landon as he laid in his bed, staring up at the ceiling, with the morning light peaking in through the blinds hanging across the window. Sleep had eluded him for most of the night as thoughts of Callie, her mother and the accident kept him from finding the peace to sleep. When he crawled out of bed just after seven, his whole body ached but his heart was the source of most of his pain. As he wandered down the hallway, the open door of Callie's room caught his eye. Unable to stop himself, he tiptoed to the door and peered in. His viewpoint from the doorway allowed him to see that the bed was made, and Callie was no where to be found. Stepping inside, his stomach dropped when his eyes landed on the vacant hangers in the closet. Moving with quick strides out of Callie's empty room and down the stairs, he quickly found his parents who were making breakfast in the kitchen.

"Mom, dad, where's Callie?" Urgency and fear rang through his voice as he stared at his parents with anticipation framing his eyes.

His parents turned to face him and the moment they did, Landon noted the sympathy washed in their eyes. And before hearing it from them, realization washed over him as his shoulders slumped as the ache in his heart grew more intense. "She's gone, isn't she?"

His father's somber features confirmed the answer even before he spoke the words. "She left about forty-five minutes ago, caught the first shuttle down the mountain. I'm sorry son."

As silence enveloped the room, a tear slipped down

Landon's cheek as he focused on the sympathy washed in his parents' eyes. Without speaking, he turned on his heel and walked briskly down the hallway, feeling the need for a dose of fresh air. After shrugging into his coat, he stepped out into the chill of the cool morning and strolled towards the swing; stopping short when he saw that the swing was already occupied.

"Callie..." Surprise enveloped her name as his eyes landed on the beautiful face that had haunted him all night.

Surprise flashed in her eyes as her head jerked up in his direction. "Landon. Hi."

The sight of her in front of him filled his heart with joy, but confusion framed his eyes as he stared down at her. "Mom and dad said you left."

She nodded in answer as tears pooled in her eyes. "I did but I turned around before I even made it off the property. I couldn't get on that shuttle."

Relief and hope flooded Landon's mind as he tilted his head and a relieved tremble danced across his lips. "Why?"

She rose from the swing, grasping a book in her hands. "Because of this and because of you."

As relieved as he was, the reality of the past hit him as he shook his head and dread filled his heart. "Callie..."

"Landon, let me talk first, please?" Her eyes, like her words were pleading with him.

Nodding slowly, he took a deep breath, preparing himself for what she was about to say.

"Okay, first I want to apologize for last night."

He immediately began shaking his head. "Callie, you don't have to. I completely understand."

"No, Landon, I do have to. I was overwhelmed and I needed a moment to process it all. But I'm sorry I pushed you away and I'm sorry if I made it seem like I was mad or that I blame you, because I don't."

Landon's eyes widened slightly as misery began to fill them and he shook his head again as his shoulders slumped and he bowed his head. "Callie, you should. I took your mother away from you."

"Landon." His name was soft off her lips. "You and I both know that it was an accident." He opened his mouth to respond but she continued, forcing him to remain quiet. "I have something I want to read to you." Opening the book that she was clutching, she flipped the pages, glancing back up at him when she found the page she was looking for. "I wrote this two years ago, on the twentieth anniversary of my mother's death."

"Callie…" A hint of misery enveloped her name as it left his lips which prompted her to offer him a pleading smile.

"Landon, let me read this, please?"

He stared at her for a moment, before nodding. When he did, she returned her focus to the open page in front of her. He watched her chest move as she took a deep breath before she began to read aloud.

"Dear stranger whose life was unknowingly intertwined with mine, twenty years ago. I was three years old that night, too young to understand what happened but I understand it now and I have for a long time. I've thought about you often over the years and my grandfather and I would often say a prayer for you. It was always the same prayer, and it was more like a wish than a prayer. He wished, we wished, that you would have a wonderful life. That the tragedy that occurred on that dark, rainy night twenty years ago, did not darken your heart or your soul. We have never blamed you." She paused and lifted her eyes up to his. There were tears brimming in the corners of them and Landon could feel tears in his own eyes as she returned her focus to the pages in front of her. "How could we blame a kid whose only mistake was being in the wrong place at the wrong time. My mother had demons. She wrestled with those demons for many years and I'm sorry that when her demons took her down, they took you down as well. One day I hope to say this to you in person." She lifted her eyes back up to his as she continued. "I'm sorry. I'm sorry that you had to live with this for the past twenty years and I just hope that it didn't destroy you, because you deserve better than that. Take care, Callie Anderson."

Landon felt a mixture of relief and pain as he stared into her eyes. "Callie…"

Shaking her head, she held her hand up to stop him. "Wait, there's more. As I sat out here on this swing this morning, I wrote another passage. This time it was a letter to you."

"Callie…" Tears choked her name as it left his lips.

She grabbed his hand, while keeping her eyes locked on his. As she stared into his eyes, he could see a mixture of hope and sadness lingering within them. "Landon, please let me read this to you and if after I'm done you want to part ways, I will completely understand but that is not what I want."

Landon's eyes widened at the conviction of her confession but before he could reply, she let go of his hand and began flipping through the book until she found the right page. She looked up at him briefly before dropping her eyes back down. When she spoke, he could hear tears enveloping her words.

"Dear Landon, I don't know what to say. Or at least I didn't know what to say. When you told me the truth, that it was you behind the wheel that night, I felt like my whole world stopped. And I lost my mother all over again but this time, it wasn't just her I lost, I lost you too. Over the past week, I have felt so much happiness being with you. A happiness that I haven't felt in a really long time and when you initially told me about that night, I felt lost. But your confession doesn't change how I feel and it doesn't change the time we've spent together. Landon, you made me feel like I belonged in a way that I haven't felt since Pops died. You made me feel the way he always did, like I'm important, like I have a place in this world. For the past seven years, I've been living a life of solitude and it's been lonely. But I didn't even realize that until I came here to your family's cabin. Here I had people to care about again and that cared about me. You have all opened your hearts to me and you Landon, you have opened my heart too. Here in this cabin, your family's Christmas cabin, you have given me the most amazing, most unexpected Christmas. I just reread the letter that I wrote to the young man that was in the car the night my mother died and everything that I wrote is still true. I'm sorry that you had to live with that guilt, with the knowledge that someone died, because it wasn't your fault and I'm sorry that my mother did that to you. I'm sorry that she did that to us. She was messed up and she made a mistake that impacted so many lives. But I think in some way, she had a hand in bringing us together. And I think that my Pops and Izzie did too."

She paused and locked her eyes onto his before continuing. "I was there at the cemetery the day you buried Izzie." She paused again as a gasp flew from his mouth. His eyes were wide as she stared up at him and he felt a shiver roll down his spine. A hint of a smile touched her lips as she continued. "I was visiting Pops and as I was leaving, I watched you and Scarlet at Izzie's grave. I didn't know it was you until the other day when you mentioned that dark, rainy October day. When I put two and two together, I was shocked, but I think it's a sign. Or maybe not a sign but destiny, like the people we loved in our pasts were helping us find each other, because Landon Pierce..." She raised her eyes up and he could see them sparkle as they latched onto his. "I'm falling in love with you."

He drew in a surprised intake of breath at her confession, prompting a smile to touch her lips. She raised her hand up to his cheek and placed it gently against his skin. "I know it's quick but it's how I feel."

Landon felt his heart dance with joy as he stared into her eyes. He took a moment to swallow the emotional lump that had begun to form in his throat, then he placed his hand against hers on his cheek. "Callie, I...I feel it to. I do, but..." Concern flooded his eyes, as reality crashed his mind, but her lips curled upwards as she threw her book down onto the swing and used her other hand to softly caress his other cheek while staring at him with loving eyes.

"Landon, no buts. What happened in the past is in the past. I never blamed that young man for the accident and I don't blame you. I couldn't. You are the most amazing man I have ever met. You are kind and generous and you have spent your entire life paying penance for an accident that wasn't your fault. Isn't it time for you to forgive yourself?"

Landon didn't respond, instead he crushed his lips against hers, letting his love for her overtake him. She responded immediately as she moved her lips with his. They wrapping their arms around each other and he pulled her close to him, needing to feel the warmth of her body against his. When they eventually pulled their lips apart, they were both breathless. Happiness washed over him as he beamed down at her. "Callie Anderson, you are an amazing woman and I'm falling in love with you too and I am so glad that you didn't get on that shuttle."

Callie's eyes sparkled and she giggled before leaning up onto her tip toes and pressing her lips against his, whispering as she did. "Me too. Merry Christmas Landon."

Love and happiness flooded through him as he responded. "Merry Christmas, Callie!"

Epilogue

Chords of Christmas carols floated through the air and the Christmas Eve Eve ball was in full swing as Landon led Callie out onto the terrace. There was a chill in the air as small flakes of fluffy white snow wafted down from the sky. As they approached the railing, Landon let his gaze focus on his beautiful date, and a fresh wave of nerves swept through his body. Callie, oblivious to the nerves that were jolting him, kept her eyes focused on the sparkling trees and white, snow-capped mountains that spanned into the distance around them.

She sighed and then spoke with a hint of awe etched in her voice. "This view will never get old. It's so beautiful."

Landon's gaze didn't waiver from her when he replied. "It certainly is."

Callie turned her eyes towards him and her sparkling pink lips curled upwards. "I was talking about the view." A hint of amusement enveloped her words.

Landon's own lips curled upwards and a twinkle touched his eyes. "So was I. My view right now is

195

amazing."

His compliment elicited a pink hue to creep across her cheeks and she dipped her eyes down, clearly embarrassed by his remark.

Placing his index finger under her chin, he brought her eyes back up to meet his. "You are the most beautiful woman I have ever seen. Have I told you that lately?"

A smile touched her eyes as she shook her head slightly. "Not in the past twenty minutes."

His eyes danced. "Well, you are." She smiled in reply and he bent his head down, pressing his lips against hers. When he straightened back up, she smiled up at him with a sparkle in her eyes before returning her gaze to the beauty around them.

As she did, Landon took a deep breath, realizing that this was the perfect moment. Reaching into his jacket pocket, he wrapped his trembling fingers around the little box resting inside and pulled it out. Taking another deep breath, he began the speech he had been rehearsing all week.

"Callie, I love you."

She turned loving eyes on him. "I love you too."

Landon's lips curled upwards. "Good, because there's something that I wanted to say, well to ask you and I thought this would be the perfect place to do it."

The love in her eyes remained but a flicker of confusion flashed across them as she tilted her head.

Landon looked down at the box in his hands and as

he did, her eyes followed. Bringing his gaze back up, he watched her eyes widened and as he opened the box to reveal the beautiful turquoise and diamond engagement ring resting inside, a gasp escaped her lips. As she brought her wide, surprised eyes up to meet his, he saw a tear shimmering within them.

"Oh my god!" The words were a hushed whisper as they left her lips.

Before she could say anything further, Landon began his speech. "Callie Anderson, I love you. And I think I have since the first moment I saw you. You are the most amazing woman I have ever met. You are kind and thoughtful, funny, and wise and so damn beautiful! And you have the most amazing spirit. I never thought that I could love after Izzie, but you opened up my world again and showed me that I could and that it could be just as amazing as it was before. And you love my daughter as much as she deserves to be loved. You love her like she's your own and she loves you just as much. You have brought so much joy into our lives over the past year. And, I want that joy to continue for the rest of our lives. I want you to be a part of our family forever." He paused and lowered himself down to one knee. "Will you marry me?"

Tears streamed down her cheeks and without hesitation, she nodded her head. "Yes, yes, of course I'll marry you."

His heart leapt as her words registered in his mind. "Really?"

"Yes." She repeated and then leaned down and pressed her lips against his. When she straightened back up, she extended her left hand out and he slipped the ring onto her finger. Then leaping up, he enveloped her in his arms, lifted her off the ground and flung her around as they both giggled with delight. As they were celebrating, he heard a commotion behind him and smiled, knowing it was his family. Setting Callie back down on the ground, he kept his arm around her waist as they turned to greet the beaming faces of his family.

A chorus of congratulations sounded around them as hugs and handshakes were exchanged and glasses of champagne were passed around. As Landon's eyes remained focus on his bride-to-be, his father raised his glass.

"To Landon and Callie. To forgiving the past and finding a new beginning."

"To Landon and Callie." The rest of the family echoed after Nick as they raised their glasses to the soon to be Mr. and Mrs. Landon and Callie Pierce."

Made in United States
Orlando, FL
02 October 2022

22917207R00125